Belinda
and the Dustbunnys

Belinda
and the Dustbunnys

by Madeline Sonik

Illustrated by Grania Bridal

A HODGEPOG BOOK

Hodgepog Books acknowledges the ongoing support of the Canada Council for the Arts.

EDITORS
Luanne Armstrong and Dorothy Woodend.

COVER DESIGN AND INTERIOR LAYOUT
Jane Lightle, Bibelot Communications.
Set in Adobe Garamond and Oswald.

Published in Canada by Hodgepog Books,
3476 Tupper Street
Vancouver, BC V5Z 3B7
604.874.1167

NATIONAL LIBRARY OF CANADA CATALOGUING IN PUBLICATION DATA
Sonik, Madeline, 1960-
    Belinda and the Dustbunnys/Madeline Sonik; Grania Bridal, illustrator

ISBN 0-9730831-4-X

I. Bridal, Grania. II. Title.
PS8587.0558B44   2003   C2003-911249-7

For my darling dancing Dyana, who skipped into my office from school each day demanding to hear the next installment of this book and who made me promise we would use its proceeds to help children find their way home.

One

Belinda lived in the attic room of a leaky, creaky, run-down house with windows that rattled when the wind blew, and sinks that ran rusty red water.

She didn't know how long she'd been here, or how old she was. She guessed she'd been here since she was a baby, because she could not remember ever having lived anywhere else. She was alone in the attic, and saw no one, except for a person called Gulch, who told Belinda she was her nursemaid. Three times a day, Gulch scaled the winding, wobbling, wooden stairs of the house, bringing tepid water and dry molding bread for Belinda to eat.

Sometimes, Belinda could scrape enough grey soot off the shaky nailed-down windows that she could see two children in a nearby yard. The children romped and played and swung on the vine-like branches of willow trees. She imagined herself with them. She imagined it so strongly that she could smell the fragrant lilac bushes, their sprays of purple blooms and the velvety maroon petals of roses that bordered the entire yard. She could feel the cool stone pathway against her feet, follow its winding outline to the sun-warmed birdbath and touch the pool of water that collected in its graceful bowl.

"Stay away from that window," Gulch snapped each time she entered the room. She was thin, long-faced, bony. Hair sprouted out of the top of her nose like little clumps of black grass and a trail of warts jiggled from the tip of her nose to her chin. She wore rough tweedy skirts and jackets and seemed perpetually uncomfortable. Grey cotton stockings clung to her pole-shaped legs, and around her waist rattled a great bunch of brass keys on a chain. She looked as threadbare and old as a worn out walking shoe, for although she was no more than eighteen years old, malevolent thoughts and evil actions had absorbed every ounce of natural beauty she had ever possessed. In people who are kind and good, natural beauty never vanishes even when they age, but in people like Gulch who resist goodness at all costs, a putrid mummification sets in.

Belinda always did as Gulch said. She did not like for her to linger. "Yes, Nursemaid Gulch, thank you, Nursemaid Gulch," she said as she took the plate of moldy crusts and the glass of lukewarm water. She scrunched her face with effort, trying to imagine Gulch as someone nicer.

"I know what you're trying to do!" Gulch croaked. A stray eye pinned Belinda under its gaze.

Belinda looked away.

"You're trying to rearrange me, aren't you?"

"No," Belinda whispered.

"Don't try it!" Gulch warned.

For many months now, Gulch had noticed a growing strength in Belinda's imagination, which troubled her. "Imaginative children are incredibly slippery," she thought.

Belinda breathed a great sigh and collapsed cross-legged on the dusty floor as soon as she was left alone. A session with Gulch was like wrestling a giant bloodsucker. But now she could relax. She could think nice thoughts and enjoy her crust of bread and water, for her imagination allowed her to enjoy the most unpleasant things.

First, she made herself very calm, and then she stared at the bread and water. She concentrated on it, gently, rather like you might concentrate on a butterfly you wished to land on the top of your head. The warm water began to bubble and froth and release rainbow-coloured steam. The bread swelled and shook and made sounds like a locomotive. The room spun, the ceiling grew, the floor trembled, and all the while Belinda sat calmly gazing at the bread and water, like you might gaze at a four-leaf clover in your garden, or a tiny hummingbird. And then, suddenly there stood before Belinda a large wooden table, covered with the most exquisite morsels of food.

"I believe I'll have the pumpkin pie today," she said, licking her lips and taking a large slice, "with cream," she added, dropping on a dollop of thick, rich whipping cream.

"Mmmmmmmmmm, tasty, very tasty. And a cup of hot chocolate too."

There were crustless sandwiches of all kinds cut into neat triangles, little cheese tarts, and potato salad, big thick slices of water-melon, and both cherry and apple pastries. There was chocolate cake and éclairs and ice cream, roast beef and fried chicken, hot apple cider, juice, milk and jars upon jars of cookies. When Belinda had had her fill, the table disappeared.

Then, in place of the miserable tatty square of blanket where she was expected to sleep, she imagined a beautiful soft bed with a thick puffy quilt. She always fell quickly asleep and always dreamed wonderful dreams. In some, she was able to slide open the dusty window of the attic, fly through the warm evening sky, and land in the yard just beyond where the children were playing. In others, she dreamed she was safe and sound, living happily in a small brick house with yellow tulips in the garden and a white picket fence. Here, there were two people who loved her, a mother and a father, and when she awoke, she was aware of a vague memory of these two round jolly faces that kissed her and called her "dear, dear, little heart." She'd try to will the faces back, to re-create them in her imagination as parents, but the memory, like a small skipping record, always ended too quickly, and instead she was left with two other faces, two nasty, twisted, thorny faces and the looming ugliness of Gulch.

When Gulch came to collect the dishes, not a crumb of moldy bread was left on the bread plate, nor a drop of warm water in the greying glass. Lately she'd been finding traces of other foods, delicious foods, like particles of pastry and chips of cheddar cheese. This troubled Gulch enormously for she and the couple who employed her were the only people who possessed keys to the attic. It was impossible for Belinda to leave and impossible for anyone to get in. "That slimy brat scares me," Gulch told her employers one evening. "She's becoming dangerous." But her employers were absorbed arguing over a game of canasta, and didn't hear a word she said.

One day, just after Gulch had dropped off the ghastly green bread and the terrible tepid water, Belinda collected all her courage and asked meekly, "Where are my parents?"

She said it so softly that it was almost inaudible, but it cut the air with such a sharp, decided swipe that it could not be ignored.

Belinda did not ask questions often, and Gulch disliked it when she did.

"You want to know about your parents?" she asked, stalling, rubbing bony fingers together until they crackled.

"Yes, please," Belinda answered, a quaver of uncertainty lodged in her voice.

"I'll tell you about them," whispered Gulch, her eyes like sharp pieces of twirling steel. "Your parents are wonderful people," she said smoothly and a grin cut across the line of her mouth. "So kind...so good." She started picking at one of her warts as she thought, and Belinda began feeling queasy. "They make you stay here in this room to protect you. They simply worship you. And you must work hard to make yourself worthy of their...love," she muttered.

"Protect me from what?" Belinda asked.

Gulch inhaled. "Oh, my dear. Have you forgotten? Have you forgotten all about the terrible, evil, black monsters that live outside? They have been searching for you for years, and I'm afraid one day they might just find you."

"Black monsters!" Belinda cried.

"Hideous, horrible monsters," Gulch said, slithering toward the window.

"They're out there," she said, "just on the other side of the glass, but very well hidden, you know."

"Really?"

"Would I lie to you?" Gulch grinned again, this time revealing nubby rotting teeth. "They live just out there, and that is why I always tell you to get away from the window. The most horrible thing would happen if you were spotted."

Belinda was aware of fear roiling and rising inside of her, lifting like the lid of a frantic bubbling pot. She didn't want to hear any more, yet she heard herself ask, "What? What will happen?"

"Why, they'd fly right at the window and shatter it to bits. You wouldn't even know what hit you. You'd just suddenly feel a rush of cold air and hear terrible noises, and the black monsters would be all over you. Gnawing away at your pretty neck, eating your ears, lapping your legs. You'd feel everything. It would be the most excruciating torture you could possibly imagine." Gulch's eyes rolled, her grin hardened. "It would be most unpleasant."

Beads of sweat were forming on Belinda's forehead and her body was refusing to stay still. Her hands were trembling like frightened herons and her feet were tapping the dust loose from the floor.

"But that isn't the worst of it," Gulch continued. "Once they're finished gluttonously gobbling you, and your body is no more than fine white skeleton dust, that part of you that's left without a body, that part that's floating about the room looking desperately for a place to go, gets sucked into their blackness, and you become one of them. There is no way out. There is no fighting it at all. You have no say in the matter whatsoever. You simply become a black monster, just like them, and roam the world doing evil. Eventually, of course, there will be no goodness left. There will be no children. And that is why your dear, thoughtful parents have put you away in this room. Because the monsters tried to get you once, and your parents are determined they don't get another chance." Belinda gulped. She didn't want Gulch to say any more, yet there was still one question burning inside of her, and she feared if she didn't ask it now, she might never have the courage to ask it later.

"If my parents do worship me, as you say they do...if they do love me, then why is it they never come to see me?"

Gulch caught Belinda on the jagged edge of her gaze.

"Shhhhhhhhhhhhhhhhhhhhhhh," she said.

"Shhhhhhhhhhh?" Belinda asked.

"Hush now," Gulch said, raising a crooked finger to her mealy lips.

"Shhhhhhhhh," she repeated before she left the room.

Belinda sat quietly after Gulch left, thinking about her parents. She'd like to believe they were good and kind, she'd like to believe they'd locked her in this lonely empty room for her own protection, yet something inside her said "it can't be true." And even though her imagination was strong, it could not erase this voice of doubt.

When Gulch closed and locked the door of the attic, her frozen smile shattered like an icicle. She hobbled down the winding, rickety stairway to a dark, heavy door, muttering curses.

It took a great deal of strength to push the door open. A small child could not do it. The light on the other side was strong and Gulch's wobbly eyes blinked. She trailed down another long flight of stairs. This stairway was covered with shabby brown carpet and at the bottom of these stairs, she stopped muttering, and wailed at the top of her lungs: "SOMEONE HAS TO GET RID OF THAT HORRIBLE BRAT!"

Two

It would be hard to imagine a person as vile and despicable as Gulch, and even if it were easy, it's unlikely that anyone would want to try. She was so foul that if she stood next to a vase of cut chrysanthemums they'd wilt. If she fixed her gaze on a gentle dog, it would whimper and run for its life. Babies out on their daily strolls cried inconsolably if Gulch so much as approached a city block of their buggies, and all objects she reached for had an odd way of shifting, as if they were recoiling from her toxic touch.

She had not always been this way though. Once, she was as nice as any little girl you see playing hopscotch in the schoolyard, or digging sand at the beach. Her name wasn't Gulch, but Genevieve and she once even had a friend, but those days were long behind her and forgotten now. She could not recall ever having been a child, and so she maintained she'd never been one. "I came out of a bog, fully grown," she told people. It began as a dark little story to frighten, and it pleased her to tell untruths then. But before long, she'd lost her way, as happens so often when truths get twisted, and she began believing her very own lies.

The reason she began lying in the first place is very sad. When Gulch was no more than seven years old, she was snatched from her parents. Her mother and father, who were quite wealthy and loved her more than anything, combed the world for her. They placed ads in newspapers from Berlin to Bangkok, New York to Nairobi, Paris to Pasadena, London to Lima. They were tireless in their effort, searching, ever searching, never stopping. They hired secret agents, employed detectives of all kinds, bought the best packs of German shepherds and bloodhounds to sniff her out, but she had disappeared without a trace. And all their efforts in all the long years had not brought her back to them. She couldn't remember her parents at all, for the criminals who snatch children make sure to do a thorough brainwashing right off, which is a most frightful operation. It is much more dangerous and painful than simply having a mouth washed out with soap. The strongest, smelliest dishwashing detergent is applied to the ears, and hot water is then washed through. The victim's head is shaken until all the wonderful, beautiful memories of people once loved are drowned and rinsed down the drain like greasy dishwater.

When the two criminals who snatched Genevieve washed her brain, she lost all memory of her happy life with her parents. She didn't know she'd been snatched. She even forgot her own name. She began to lie to fill in the gap left in her brain where all her remembers had been stored, and the lies, like weeds in an untended garden, multiplied at such an alarming rate that Gulch even forgot what were lies and what were truths.

Another side effect was that Gulch's eyes, always steady and truthful, began to wobble and wibble and jiggle about. That was because the slimy, slippery dishwashing detergent was never completely rinsed clear. And sometimes, when Gulch thought too hard, or for too long a time, tiny white bubbles would drip from her ear holes, looking exactly like foam on a mad dog's mouth. Brainwashing is such a painful operation and happens so quickly that one can't even cry over what's been lost, for as soon as it's gone it's completely forgotten. The victim walks about feeling as empty as a broken milk bottle, as hollow as an echo, without knowing why. It is a most frustrating and infuriating thing, and when the victim begins to build a new life for herself — even if it is formed on a foundation of lies — it is always built with the fear it may be snatched away at any moment.

Over the years the lies ate up every good thought in Gulch's head. Where she might have developed feelings, there was a collection of hard, brittle lies lodged that stopped the natural flow of blood and gave her face a wan, green-blue tinge.

She hated small animals and truly despised children, for whenever she saw one, she felt the lies rumbling, and it made her quite dizzy. Secretly, she feared one day the lies might slip and kill her.

The criminals who brainwashed Gulch sold her to a woman called Mavis, who was desperate to have a daughter of her own to mold. She had definite ideas of what she'd plant in a daughter and what she'd rip out. She wanted absolutely no defiance, and absolutely strict obedience. She wanted absolutely no untidiness, noisiness, clumsiness or foolishness. She expected her daughter to be prompt, polite, grateful and, above all, dutiful. She didn't really care where this daughter came from, and she had lots of money so she didn't mind paying a good price for one. She'd tried to legally adopt a daughter but was told "moulding" a child wasn't a good enough reason to get one.

She was indignant then. "I shall get a daughter, and I shall be the most perfect mother that ever was — you wait and see!" she snapped at social workers and lawyers.

It was surprising that she didn't always treat Gulch badly. In fact, at times, she treated Gulch quite well, but only when Gulch behaved exactly as she was told.

If for a moment Gulch forgot her manners, or spilled her milk, or forgot to tuck her shirttail into her skirt, then it was as if she'd unleashed a demon in Mavis.

She'd jump up and down like a monkey in her spiky-heeled shoes, screaming and shouting and beating Gulch over the head with a rolled up newspaper. "What do I have to do..." Mavis would screech, batting Gulch, "to get it through your head," she'd yowl, her eyes bulging "...that you're not to be imperfect! I can't abide imperfection! Do you understand?"

Gulch would nod her head. She couldn't even cry when things like this happened. The brainwashing detergent had taken its toll and clogged up her tear ducts. All she could do was let her eyes roll around aimlessly.

Another thing Mavis was unceasingly strict about and which perhaps caused the most damage was that Gulch must always live in a purely factual world.

"No good being brought up in a world of fairies and Easter bunnies, my girl. The sooner you learn to do without those things, the better."

The same with toys. Not so much as a yo-yo was allowed in the house. Once, Gulch had made the mistake of asking for a baby doll she'd seen in a department store while Mavis was trying on perfectly pressed dresses.

"It's not a real baby," Mavis had said contemptuously, "it's just a pretend doll! Why on earth would you want an ugly thing like that!"

Mavis never stopped to ask herself what happens to a child's imagination if you plug it up. She never pondered over where imperfect pieces go. And if you were to tell her all these things she'd cut out of Gulch, like bad spots in an apple, didn't just vanish, but banded together in the blackest, darkest, vilest places, developing strength and life and energy all their own, she would have simply said, "You are wrong!" and probably made some comment about the stain on your shirt, or the crooked crease in your pants.

Needless to say, not too many years passed before Mavis couldn't stand the sight of Gulch and wanted to be rid of her. "I believe you are the most imperfect creature that ever walked the face of the earth, and on top of it, you've grown quite ugly," Mavis said one night at the dinner table. Gulch gave up trying to please Mavis. She chewed her food audaciously, opening her mouth wide, letting bits fall in front of her. When dinner was over she belched so loudly, crystal wine glasses shattered.

"I hate you," she muttered at Mavis, "If I knew how, I'd turn you into a pillar of salt." She fixed her wonky eyes on Mavis. Mavis felt the small hairs on the back of her neck stand at attention and try to run.

"I suppose I shouldn't have expected any better from a foundling child!" Mavis cried. "Obviously, your parents gave you away because you were so miserable."

The next day Mavis dragged Gulch by the ear out of her house and down the street to a taxi cab, which took them all the way across two cities to the home of Cedric and Theodora Dustbunny.

After a great deal of arguing with Mavis, Cedric agreed to take Gulch back.

"In future," Theodora shouted when Mavis had left, "you must make it clear we don't take returns!"

"I made it clear!" Cedric yelled, his face as purple and wrinkled as an aging eggplant, "but she said she was going to call the police. We can't have that."

12

"Now there's another mouth to feed!" Theodora persisted, "and an ugly one. We won't be able to sell her again. She's grown too old. No one will want her."

"Well, at least the old ferret didn't demand her money back," Cedric said.

"No…but who's stuck with the hideous child now? Children are very expensive to feed and clothe. They have this terrible habit of growing. You should have demanded more money, Cedric. You're an idiot! By taking her back, you've set a precedent. Now everyone and their dog will think they can bring back children. They'll take advantage — you mark my words."

"You're overreacting," Cedric said.

"Tell me what we'll do with her then? How's she going to earn her keep? We don't have any cornfields to hang her in."

"I'm sure we could teach her to be useful around the house. Let's face it, Theodora, you've never been much with a mop or broom."

And so it was that Gulch was put to work in the large, old, crumbling house, scrubbing soiled black floors that had not been cleaned in a hundred years, scraping scummy steel pots and pans that had only ever been rinsed with cold water and were caked with hardened slop, swabbing sludgy, smelly toilets that had never known toilet brushes, and the worst chore of all — looking after the repulsive brat called Belinda,

"That brat will be the ruin of us, madam," Gulch now told Theodora Dustbunny. Theodora had put her playing cards away and was lounging on the worn chesterfield, feeding an assemblage of meat-eating plants chunks of steak and filing her nails to sharp white points.

"Shut up, Gulch! You give me a headache," Theodora droned.

Gulch fell silent, her wobbling eyes stopped moving.

"Oh, go ahead and tell me why the child's upset you," Theodora sighed.

"She's asking questions, madam," Gulch gasped. "She wants to know why her parents don't visit."

"Ah," Theodora responded, extending her hands like two five-pointed stars.

"What am I to say?" Gulch tried not to raise her voice.

"Say? I don't know. Tell her they're sick. Yes, that's it, say they have malaria. They're incapacitated. For goodness sake, I don't know. Can't you think of anything yourself? You really are a worthless black sack of ugliness, Gulch."

"Yes, madam," Gulch said.

Belinda had never been downstairs in the house, or if she had, she certainly didn't remember. Locked away in the attic, she was far removed from the daily squabbles and discord. She could hear nothing beneath her; she could not even see the side of the house through the spot she scratched clean in the dirty attic window. There was no reason for her to imagine where Nanny Gulch vanished to when she left the attic, no reason to concern herself over what might be occurring down below, nothing to intrude upon her burgeoning imagination. Unfettered, Belinda's imagination could do the most remarkable things.

If she had been able to see the sides of the house and her thoughts had not gotten weighed down wondering what was going on and why, she might not have been able to slip out the window, as carefree as a clam, into the beautiful world where she longed to be.

Very few people in the world have ever successfully used their imagination to transport themselves from one place to another. And if you were to suggest to a scientist this was even possible, he'd laugh himself silly. But the fact was Belinda had spent so much time working with her imagination, since time and imagination were all she had, that she had become as skilled with it as any professional athlete becomes skilled in the use of her body.

She had even developed her own formula, which required

imagination, concentration, desire and faith. It is, however, difficult to know in what proportions, and the skill lies in learning how to measure these things accurately.

It didn't happen all at once, though. Any kind of mastery is a process of trial and error. And for Belinda, it was no different. She would accidentally stumble on successes, like sand dollars on the beach, and sometimes things went abysmally wrong.

Her first real breakthrough was when she discovered she could actually taste the ice cream the children next door were eating.

"There must be something in this," she thought then, and focused her concentration, and sat back softly and sighed. She let her body become like a lighthouse, shining her across and over, for it is one thing to imagine a banquet out of bread and water, and another completely to imagine yourself through time and space. It is a very delicate operation that requires the utmost in concentration, for if your concentration is not a steady, constant stream, if it breaks for one moment, or surges suddenly at the wrong time, you may find yourself tumbling through thin air to awake on the ground with a broken arm or worse.

Luckily, this never happened to Belinda. But she did find, especially at first, that transporting herself took lots of energy and exhausted her.

If Belinda had not been stuck in that barren attic, if she had been a child with things about to distract her, it is most likely she would never have developed her gift. Most people do not like to work themselves to exhaustion, and if they happen to do it once, they rarely do it again. They never give themselves the chance to learn that the next time is always easier.

But Belinda learned this early on with some of her first experiments in transforming rotten bread and water. Back then, she wouldn't have been strong enough to attempt to move through splotchy, dirty glass, let alone try to join the children in the yard next door. But, over time, she felt her ability develop. She felt stronger and more powerful. And then, one day, as she calmly watched the children playing, she felt their horrified eyes upon her. They had spotted her watching them, not from behind a clear spot in the old, smoky window, but rather hovering in front of it like an opaque child-shaped kite.

Three

The children who lived next door were twins named Jill and Jerry. They had been playing a game of croquet, but now they were staring up at Belinda, who appeared more like a ghost than a girl. It was difficult for Belinda to hover like that, and she was only able to sustain herself for a few moments before she grew weak and had to imagine herself back inside the attic. When she vanished, the two children shot into their house.

"I hope I haven't scared them," Belinda worried, but comforted herself imagining that soon she would be right down there with them, explaining what had happened.

The children raced to their mother sputtering and crying. "A ghost," Jerry wheezed. "Next door," Jill added.

Their mother was doing some mending. "My goodness, you haven't been hitting each other with your croquet mallets again, have you?" She looked up from a bundle of play clothes and patches, and a cookie tin of buttons that clattered like beans.

Once, when the twins had both wanted the red mallet, they had hit each other so hard they had become absolutely giddy.

"No, Mother. For real. Honestly. Cross my heart, hope to die, stick a needle in my eye," Jerry recited.

"Well, I don't think we need to go that far," their mother said. She put her bundle of mending down and touched their faces. "You're awfully hot," she said. "I hope you haven't caught too much sun."

She brought two wet cloths for their foreheads and made them lie down in their beds for the rest of the afternoon, which was not fun for them at all. And the next morning, before she did anything else, she went out and bought two hats to protect them from the sun.

"I don't know if I want to go out and play croquet today," Jerry said to Jill. Jill knew Jerry was scared. Twins seldom can keep secrets from each other.

"Well, I'm going out," Jill said. "I'm going to try and find that ghost again and ask her what she's doing here. I read in a book ghosts are only parts of people that don't know they're dead yet. Maybe if I tell her she's dead, she'll leave."

"Maybe she'll make you a ghost too," Jerry said, his voice quivering

"Ghosts don't kill people, silly — anyway, she didn't really look all that fierce."

The two crept into their back yard as if it were pitch dark outside, taking small hesitant steps. They were afraid to look up at the attic window next door.

"Is she there?" Jerry asked.

"I don't see her," Jill whispered.

Belinda watched from behind her window. "What new game can this be?" she thought as the twins crept and hid behind bushes in their yard.

Her gaze fell upon them as softly as an eyelash, and she relaxed and sighed deeply and began her gentle concentration. "I would like to play with them, perhaps today I will be able to, perhaps today I just might," she thought calmly.

Slowly, very slowly, the window began to creak and rattle. The air around it became hazy violet. The wall groaned. Belinda felt her small body shake. From the corner of her eye she saw a flash, and then another, swirling lights that spun one way, turned red, orange, and yellow, and then spun in the opposite direction turning green, turquoise, and gold.

"It's working," she thought, "it's working." Her hair flew as if she were facing a cyclone. Her heart felt as if it was turning somersaults. Her body was becoming feather light. It was becoming feather small. It was discombobulating. It was transfiguring, and she, Belinda, was living every minuscule change, every tiny translation.

Belinda was having a much more powerful reaction transporting herself this time, and it was taking much longer. If you've ever played catch you'll know that when you throw a ball a short distance it's over and done with in a moment, but when you wind back to hurl a ball across an entire park, it requires much more effort. So it was with Belinda. Her imagination was strong enough now to take aim a long way off. But it was not entirely smooth sailing. As she moved into the dusty glass, a jolting crash rang in her ears, and a thud as loud as the sky falling transfixed her. She knew immediately things were not right and

willed herself back. Just one more second and she would have been stuck forever in the centre of the smudgy glass, like some indistinguishable black particle. Instead, she was at the bottom of the windowsill, no larger than a speck of dust. It requires an incredible amount of strength to stop the imagination when it's in progress. And once it's stopped, there's no telling if it will start up immediately again. Belinda wasn't sure at first where she was. The acrid scent of Nursemaid Gulch was creeping through the air. And suddenly she understood what had happened: Gulch must have entered the attic just as she was about to move through the glass.

"Where are you?" Gulch croaked.

Her words were like hurricanes to the tiny Belinda, who held onto a thin splinter of wood at the sill, so she wouldn't be blustered away.

Although Gulch was as thick as the fleece on a herd of sheep, even she could see there was no place for Belinda to hide in the empty attic — no bed to hide under, no closet to hide in, no toys or clothes to pull around herself like an invisible cloak. The only thing there was in the cold, damp room was Belinda's small, tattered sleeping blanket, and any fool, including Gulch, could see that even a child as skinny as Belinda could not hide under such a scrap.

"Come out this instant!" Gulch persisted. "At once, do you hear?"

Belinda did hear. She heard all too well. Gulch's words swelled like tidal waves and whipped like raging winds. "COME OUT THIS INSTANT." The words bounced Belinda away from her sliver. She felt herself airborne and clutched at another dusty spiky branch, as her legs blew out behind her. The words rang and reverberated and buzzed through her brain.

"I'm trying," she called back, but she made less noise than the flick of a star going on at night. Gulch paced the room, her breath as hot as typhoid fever. For weeks she had turned and spun each night, instead of sleeping.

In spite of what Theodora had said, Gulch knew that as Belinda grew older and more inquisitive she also was becoming a greater threat. Theodora forbade her to say any more about this, and so it went underground and gnawed at Gulch's skin from the inside out.

Her snaggly eyes twirled like a New Year's Eve party favour. Her thin lips twitched. She knew how to come by poison. She had cleaned this house for years and had read the list of every chemical on the back of every cleanser. She knew the warnings by heart: "IF SWALLOWED, INDUCE VOMITING." "IF SWALLOWED CALL AN AMBULANCE." "IF SWALLOWED, SAY GOODBYE."

She cooked up a cauldron of cocoa. "No child can resist cocoa," she said, pouring in bottles and boxes of the most noxious poisons, turning it blue with drain cleaner and greasy with gasoline. The pot flamed and hissed. "It's ready," she muttered, "it's ready."

She put a metal ladle into the pot, but it got eaten up by the fire. "An oven proof cup," she chirped.

She had carried the cup of poisoned cocoa in her spidery hand all the way up the rickety rackety stairs to Belinda's attic. Now she could feel the hot cocoa eating its way through the cup and into her skin, and she grumbled and mumbled how the poison would be wasted.

Belinda fought the cyclone of Gulch's words that sucked at her like vacuum teeth. If it had not been for the place she'd found for herself, surrounded by dust, she would most certainly have been sniffed right up into Gulch's menacing nostril, then been sneezed right out again and splattered everywhere. The thought made her skin pucker. Pieces of fine, flaky dust smaller than herself slid up like white glitter in a snow globe. For the first time, she noticed the world around her, and it looked very much like a crumbled city suffering the worst winter of its history.

"What will I do?" Belinda said sadly. Everything had become strangely quiet, but then she heard a loud rasping wheeze.

"Who's there?" Belinda cried. She was not aware she still clung to the solid branch she had found in the storm, but just then she was made suddenly and horribly aware of it, when the branch began to shake.

Confused, Belinda still clung to the branch trying to force it to remain where it was.

The branch flicked with such power that Belinda fell. She saw then that at the end of the branch was a claw, and that a hideous creature larger than herself was attached to the branch and was emerging from a heap of dust. The creature was in fact a dust mite — a microscopic being several thousand times smaller than the head of a pin, and the branch Belinda had been holding was one of its eight thick legs.

Belinda screamed. The fine blond hairs on her arms bristled. A chill ran up and down her spine. The creature's hard black body case was dome-shaped, armoured and fearsome. Dust hung all over it like moss on a tree. It had no eyes, and its mouth and nose, which were one and the same, had four large, horrible piercing fangs. It dropped its head to the sill and began drooling over grey crumbs of dust, making the most repulsive sounds, turning the crumbs to liquid.

It lumbered towards Belinda where she stood stone still, petrified and gazing. A moment later, she was running across the windowsill faster than she could go, feeling like a piece of tissue paper blowing through the streets on a windy day. Her legs moved so quickly, her own speed seemed to create a wind that propelled her.

She had no idea where she was going. She wondered what would happen when she came to the end of the windowsill, which she was certain must happen soon. But she didn't travel as far as she believed, for when you are as small as a piece of dust even an inch seems like a very, very long way off. She had traveled less than an eighth of an inch when her foot plunged into a dust dune that gave a shriek that made her tumble off her feet. She hit the ground hard, and tiny, feathered particles danced upwards, encircling her head like a halo. That was the last thing she recalled before everything went dark and she began to dream she was playing croquet with the children next door.

Belinda sighed in her sleep. The children next door had given her the red croquet mallet. How they were laughing together. How the lovely warm sun filtered through the large, swaying poplars in their yard. How the small sparrows sang. How soft the green grass was under her bare feet. She was so very happy and knew that she was dreaming, yet she swung her mallet back and looked way, way past the line of hoops that extended all the way to the lilac bushes enclosing the yard. She hit the ball. It seemed to travel a very great distance into the yard next door and kept rolling. Suddenly, she understood something she hadn't understood before. "This is exactly what I need to do to get to the children. I need to imagine myself further than I intend, into the yard beyond theirs, and that way I will have enough energy and concentration to carry me to the place I really want to be." As she thought this, rain began to crash down into her dream. Her face was becoming wetter and wetter, but her body stayed dry. If she had woken, for a moment, she would have discovered that she had stumbled into a nest of dust mites, and one of these frightening creatures, was moving its sharp, moist mouth blindly over her face.

Four

The world we call Earth teems with worlds, worlds of miniature fungi and one-celled animals, worlds of bacteria so small that billions can hide in the lines of your hands. Dust mites are larger than this, but impossible to see without a microscope. They live everywhere, even in the cleanest homes, feasting on particles of dry dead skin. They are related to spiders and resemble them in many ways. However, 140,000 dust mites can live in an ounce of dust and even though we can't see them, the fluid they excrete from their mouths to dissolve food can make people break out in rashes and wheeze. That is why Belinda, who knew nothing of dust mites, began sniffling in her sleep. Her nose began itching in her dream. The children next door retreated to their house.

"Wake up Belinda!" they shouted from a window. "Wake up!" The rain continued falling unpleasantly on her face. It continued to irritate her nose and eyes.

"ACHHHOOO!" Belinda sneezed once, and then she sneezed again. She sneezed again so hard that she shook herself awake. Her red, runny eyes opened to find the monstrous head of a dust mite lowering its damp, frightful mouth towards her.

Belinda screamed and raised her hands to her face. She was certain whatever this monster was it was going to make her its lunch. However, the creature scuttled away. It hid in a grey, crumbly corner. Belinda sat up. She wiped her wet, sticky face with a fraying sleeve and sneezed. She rubbed her red stinging eyes. Flaky hills of dry dead skin and ropes of broken hair surrounded her. It was such a strange place to be, at the bottom of a grey dusty window, and it looked nothing like it had when Belinda was her normal size. A wind came up again. Tiny glittering dust particles began whipping through the air. She stood and planted herself as firmly as she could but felt her feet rising from the ground. She lifted her head against the wind briefly. Dust mites rolled like tumbleweeds, then spun, suspended in mid-air.

Belinda was too small to see that it was Gulch creating this enormous breeze. After she'd disposed of the searing poison she'd walked up the creaking, cracking stairs to the attic, staggering and wobbling, her face as withered as a ten-year-old prune. She'd put her old rusty key into the big, clunky lock on Belinda's door. Even her thoughts were unwieldy and jarring, for she was certain the Dustbunnys would throw her out now, and then what would become of her?

Gulch had lived with the Dustbunnys since Mavis had disowned her; they were the only family she'd ever known. Even the grottiest, grimiest orphanage wouldn't have anything to do with her now. She picked at the warts on her nose and wondered. The streets were a terrifying prospect, for Gulch had not been outside since she lived with the Dustbunnys, and every passing year she remained inside, the more afraid of the streets she became.

Her eyes whirled round in their sockets and sadly sank shut. Two tepid, shrivelled drops formed in them, and for the first time she could recall, she shed a single tear.

She wiped it hastily from her eye with the sleeve of her prickly tweed jacket and noticed its reddish tinge, like the water that sat in the old rusty taps of the house.

"It's that brat's fault!" she muttered. "I knew she was dangerous. I should have poisoned her long ago. It would have been easy then. I would have told madam she'd died of a broken heart. It would have been simple."

Gulch's cracked voice echoed in the empty room. Her large, flat foot hit the ground hard, splintering a floorboard, making big black beetles scuttle. She leapt up and down, trying to squash as many beetles as she could. "I hate her! I hate her! I hate her!" she shrieked.

And then Gulch did a very peculiar thing. She took off her big, black shoe and began hitting herself in the head with it. "Take that, you worthless, ugly cretin," she shouted at herself, her eyes spinning furiously with each blow. "And that! You...you...lizard!" she screamed, walloping herself against the wall with such force that plaster fell from the ceiling above her. "You don't deserve to be alive!" she shouted.

As she said this, a brilliant idea came to her. An idea, she thought, which would rid her of all her troubles. She would take a running leap from the door, and throw herself clear out of the grimy attic window.

"It will be magnificent," she mumbled, "it will be exactly what I deserve!"

Her flat feet slapped the wooden floor like plasticine, her knobby knees bowed, and she dashed her spindly body full speed toward the dark window. But just as she reached the glass, her wobbling eyes happened to focus through the tiny crack in the grime. Gulch recoiled, for instantly she saw below something she had hoped she would never see again — children! And as if seeing children alone wasn't bad enough, these two children looked happy and loved and not lonely at all.

Gulch felt a prickly lump form in her throat and drop to her stomach. "Ghastly!" she hissed, trying to control her eyes long enough to shut them. But her eyes refused to shut.

She tried to pull her body away from the window. She tried to run from the room, but something greater within her took control and forced her to gape. She began to chisel away at the grime on the window with long, warty fingers.

If only Gulch had known that Belinda was right under her thumb on the windowsill and was suffering terribly with each careless flick of grime, she would have doubled her efforts to make it twice as miserable,

and would have taken some pleasure in the task. She did not like to look at happy children. If you have ever eaten worms, you will know exactly how she felt. Something horrible was slithering sickeningly in her stomach, and she wanted to burp five hundred times and let it crawl out. But she could not stop herself from looking.

The wind was increasing by the second for Belinda on the windowsill, and pieces of sharp dust pummeled her. She dropped to her belly and stuck her nails into the spongy, flaky surface. Heavy pieces of thick fluff hit her face. She was losing her grip. Her sweating fingers were slipping as the ground she held onto gave way like sand in water. Then Belinda thought she must be dreaming again, for she was twirling like a little seed pod in the air and being carried as if on an ocean wave, up and down, very gently, swimming in warm, glittering light.

She tried to gain some control and found if she moved her legs as if she were running, she could slow herself down, and if she put them straight together, she would move faster. She put her head down to her knees, and found she could do a somersault in midair. She arched her back slightly, and found herself doing a full back flip. By extending her right leg and arm she could propel herself to the left, and by extending the left leg and arm, she could shift her body to the right.

She began to enjoy herself. She was enjoying herself so much she didn't even notice how long it was taking for her to reach the ground — wherever that might be. But when the ground finally did come into view, she had become such an accomplished flyer, she was able to aim for a clump of spongy fibres and land.

She licked a finger and held it up to feel for wind, but here she could feel no wind at all. "I think I've fallen into a safe little crack in the skirting board," she said aloud, surprised at how strange and squeaky her voice sounded at this size. Her scratchy nose and itchy eyes were beginning to feel less irritated, and she thought she'd better figure out a way to return to her normal size before any more dust mites started licking her face and before any more wind currents relocated her.

Five

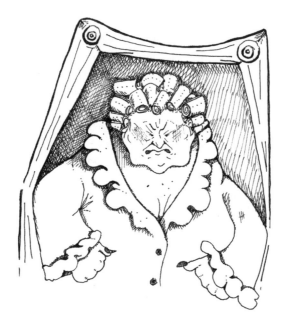

Gulch left the attic, her mind hatching a horrendous plan. In the kitchen she muttered and ran cold water for her sore, blistered fingers. "I told madam, but she wouldn't listen. Now I'll just have to replace the brat. That's all there is to it," she hissed.

The kitchen sink quivered and the water seemed compelled to avoid her smoldering fingers.

"She has no one but herself to blame," Gulch continued sullenly. "She can't blame me. It's not my fault. I tried to warn her."

"Warn her of what?" Theodora Dustbunny purred. "And who is 'her'?"

Gulch's warts throbbed and her withered head shook. Her pale green flesh turned blue, and her eyes rolled round and round like small, hard spinning marbles.

"Cat got your tongue?" Theodora asked, her sagging face invading the kitchen, looking for all the world like a fallen cake.

Gulch examined her trembling, poison-blistered hands, then the small cobwebby window over the sink as her flat feet and spindly legs tried to launch her.

"Not so fast," Theodora roared, sticking a foot out in front of Gulch. "You haven't answered my questions." Her wide powerful body stood squarely in the centre of the doorway.

Gulch plunged over Theodora's foot, hurtling through the air like a large tweed-covered bat.

"I'm sorry, madam," she blurted, as she hit the wall. "I don't know how she got away."

"Got away?" Theodora thundered, "GOT AWAY! Surely you don't mean....You can't mean.... It's impossible...not the child!" Her face contorted and twisted and almost seemed to bubble like a pot of boiling soup.

"I don't know where she's gotten to. I've searched the attic. She's not there."

Theodora grabbed hold of two black frying pans and brought them down like cymbals on Gulch's ears. "Find her!" Theodora bellowed.

Gulch's eyes whirled and gyrated, her ears rang, her brain clanged, she tried to focus on Theodora, but it was no use. She nodded quietly. She had no idea where to begin looking for Belinda and was too afraid to ask if another couple of children might not do just as well.

The rickety old front door screamed open and Cedric Dustbunny, a small, round, greasy man, entered the house in a cloud of cigar smoke. Both Gulch and Theodora grew silent.

Cedric looked at his solid gold watch and limped towards the kitchen. "Where's my dinner!" he howled. The toes on his left foot had all turned black. Whenever Gulch did the laundry, she would find toes in his socks. He'd scowl, and his slate black centipede eyebrows would meet in the middle of his forehead. "Gimme my toes, slimeball," he'd mutter. Gulch had to hand over these horrible smelly toes, no matter how disgusted she was. Cedric would stop whatever he was doing and glue them back onto his foot with Epoxy, just as if it were the most natural thing in the world.

He made money in contemptible ways. He particularly liked doing things that made people suffer. He got money from the government to run an old homeless people's home where only the most ancient and abandoned old people stayed. He'd limp through the home with his cane, and if great, great, great grandmas in their wheelchairs got in his way, he'd hit them. He fed them the most horrible slop, made from things so revolting that the mere mention of the ingredients would cause sickness. And every afternoon at a quarter to three, he forced all the inmates to go into the auditorium where he would call them insulting names and frighten them by saying he would turn them into dog food if they weren't careful. He rigged up a powerful loudspeaker so everyone could hear, and bolted the doors so everyone had to stay until he'd finished talking. He also owned several run-down apartment buildings with broken windows and cracked floors, and poison paint on the walls that chipped off when you touched it. These buildings had rats and mice and cockroaches as large as your fist running through them. Cedric never once did anything to fix them because he knew he didn't have to. The people who lived in his building were too poor to live anywhere else. He just let the buildings get worse and worse and took pleasure in his tenants' hopelessness.

He had been in a good mood thinking about the power he had to bring misery, but as he walked through the door, he heard the commotion and limped angrily off to the kitchen. He struck Gulch several times with his walking stick because she still lay dizzily against the wall blocking his passage, and he gave Theodora a jab for good measure. When Gulch finally told him that Belinda was missing, his walking stick seemed to take on a life of its own, scourging and flaying every glass and dish in sight.

"Can't you do anything right? Do I have to do everything?" he screamed. He butted his cigar in the centre of Gulch's forehead. "Don't stand around here, you fools, comb the house, search the city. Children don't just grow on trees!"

Stunned panic broke into mindless motion as everyone in the kitchen began running in different directions. Gulch left the kitchen through the back door, Theodora descended to the cellar, and Cedric raced out the front door and into his rusting Cadillac.

No one went to check the attic, for if they had, they would have found Belinda, serenely standing by the window, concentrating on transporting herself beyond the yard next door, for she had wasted no time.

She had calmed her mind, and thought of the attic room, its cobwebs and its splintery floorboards. She thought of its grimy window and the small, worn piece of blanket she slept on at night. She imagined herself her proper size standing there. It took so much of her energy to concentrate, to hold the image of the room lightly in her mind without a demand in her heart, but she was growing stronger with every thought.

Dust swirled and purple lightning flashed, and particles of dirt dropped and rumbled and crumbled around her. Her body vibrated. Her skin turned electric blue. She could feel it stretch and expand like bread dough. She could feel her head shooting up and her feet rumbling and growing beneath her. And then, suddenly, a loud, ear-smashing pop, and she found herself standing on the old rough familiar floor of the attic.

She didn't even stop to wipe the dust off herself. The twins were playing croquet, and the warm sun was dancing through the starry purple flowers of the lilac bushes.

But, just then, out of the corner of her eye she caught sight of a dark, pointed shadow, like a witch's hat, stealing alongside the children's house, casting blackness like a smoggy eclipse over a trellis of sweet peas that instantly began wilting and withering.

Belinda's knuckles tightened around the window frame, her face pressed hard against the glass. Her heart dropped into the pit of her stomach, as her mouth slowly formed the horrible name — "Gulch!"

If you've ever had to look at something ugly or sad that you would rather not see, like a dead animal in the middle of the highway, then you will know how Belinda felt when she saw Gulch's shadow and imagined her face. She wanted to cover her eyes, or look the other way. But when something wants to be in your mind, it's next to impossible to get rid of it.

Belinda tried to think of happy things, of sunlight and lilacs, of the children next door laughing and playing croquet, but Gulch's ugly face continued to grow in Belinda's mind like the sharp, thorny spikes of a blackberry bush. Belinda didn't panic, though. She took a deep breath instead. "What could it be?" she wondered. "What could she want?" Gulch's contorted face seemed absolutely gleeful in Belinda's imaginings.

Belinda sat on the dusty floor. She shut her eyes, and as clearly as she could she focused on the image of Gulch that grew ever clearer and stronger. "What are you thinking, Gulch?" she asked. "What evil are you concocting?"

To Belinda's amazement, she found herself tuning into Gulch's thoughts, just as if Gulch were an electrical transmitter and she were a transistor radio. At first, the reception was fuzzy, but soon Gulch's thoughts were pouring out loudly, like a jumbled string of pictures. They flashed on the screen of Belinda's mind, a sad and sorry slide show.

She saw two nasty-looking, vaguely familiar people: an apish, limping, greasy man with a cigar in his mouth, and a large, scrunched-face woman in a flouncey pink housedress. She saw the couple beating Gulch with sticks. She saw Gulch looking through the window of the attic room. She saw the children next door. She saw Gulch see the children next door, and then she saw Gulch grin. She saw Gulch's blistered fingers extending. Two immense burlap sacks dropped suddenly over the children as they screamed and fought for freedom.

Six

erry and Jill rested their croquet mallets against a fat oak tree and sat down on the grass. They were both bored and wanted to do something really exciting.

"Why don't we sneak next door," Jill said, "and try to find the ghost."

Even though she'd been scared ever since she'd seen Belinda at the window, she'd been itching to get inside the creaky, rickety house and investigate.

"We can't just go into someone's house. That's illegal," Jerry said. "And besides, maybe the ghost hates kids."

"I don't think so. It looked like a little girl ghost to me. I'll bet she's just lonely."

As they talked, they were unaware that just eight feet away, at the side of their house, stood a sinister presence.

"Wouldn't it be something," Jill said, "to have a real live ghost for a friend?"

"Ghosts aren't alive — they're dead, that's what makes them ghosts, silly," Jerry said, stooping to gather some dry old leaves to toss at Jill.

Jill went after Jerry then, playfully pushing him to the ground. She collected handfuls of grass, and stuffed it down his shirt.

"Stop," he yelled. "Quick, I hear something."

Jill didn't pay any attention. He'd said things like that before so he could get away from her.

"I'm not falling for that this time," she laughed. "This time, I'm going to...."

But before she was able to finish her threat, a scratchy voice floated over her head and into her ears.

"Don't be afraid, children," it whispered, "I'm not going to hurt you...."

Gulch crept forward from the shadows, her hideous eyes a swirl of whirlpools, her black teeth gleaming jet. "Come here, girl...," she whined at Jill, "...and see what I have in this big sack for you."

Jill saw the two sacks outstretched, the ugly stranger's blistered hands.

"Don't be frightened," Gulch called in her voice of curdled honey, "Santa Claus carries sacks just like these, come and see the wonderful presents."

Gulch came closer. Her legs moved nimbly like a jumping spider's. "Come see what I have for you."

"Go away!" Jill screamed. "We don't want your presents." She pulled at her brother's shirtsleeve. He was still wiping the last remnants of grass from his face.

"Now, now," Gulch said, "don't be difficult. Come, look." She hurried towards them. Jill scrambled to her feet and grabbed desperately at Jerry. "Get up!" she shouted, but Jerry didn't seem to hear. His eyes were glued to the attic window next door.

Gulch's bony hands were strong from scrubbing and cleaning, and she reached down with a snake's quickness and grabbed Jerry's leg.

"Leave my brother alone!" Jill screamed. She kicked Gulch in the shins and scratched her horrible, green flesh and grabbed for the bag, which was now tightly closed and knotted in Gulch's fist, and from which she could hear her poor brother cry.

Gulch caught Jill's wrists. "Let me go," Jill wailed, trying to wiggle free from the vise-like grip. The second sack was right up to her waist. It seemed impossible for her to get away, and then suddenly from the attic window Jill noticed a strong, bright light, almost like a moonbeam, descending. The light moved in a thin trickle and puddled right behind Gulch, who was trying to force Jill's head into the sack.

"Drop dead," Jill shouted, flinging the entire weight of her body against Gulch, forcing her to lose balance, stumble over the puddle of white light, and fall like a bowling pin.

Gulch lay on the grass, her eyes rolling every which way. "No matter what trick you're playing, girl, I will get you," she shouted at Jill. But Jill was seeing the cloudy white light rapidly gaining form.

Jill couldn't take her eyes off it. It was swelling and shaping and shading. It was now blunted and now pointed. It was even branching.

"Your silly tricks won't hurt me," Gulch cackled, as she stood. "You're just a small child, an insignificant piece of flesh!" She lunged at Jill then, catching her by the throat. "You won't get away this time," she screeched, "at least not alive." Her steely grasp was harder and more menacing than before. Jill choked for air. The world around her was rapidly growing dim.

Seven

When Belinda saw the danger the children next door were in, she instinctively went to help them.

Transporting herself did not take the great effort it had in the past, for fear and danger has a way of focusing and increasing concentration automatically. To Belinda, it felt as if she'd just slipped through the window, and she found herself standing directly behind Gulch.

Jill was swaying weakly and no longer struggling. Belinda realized Gulch had to be overpowered. She grabbed Gulch by the neck and gave it a good twist as Jill fell completely out of sight, right into the burlap sack.

Gulch moaned as Belinda fought her, but she knotted the sack and held it tight, refusing to let it go.

"Let them out," Belinda shouted, clutching now at Gulch's waist. Gulch was as angry as a wasp in a small, wet jar. She bucked Belinda up and down and all across the yard, until finally Belinda's sweating hands began to slip and her small body shot sky high. All she could see of the earth was Gulch's malevolent grinning face, turning to look. But something odd was happening. Belinda was tumbling to the ground slowly. She was fluttering down, like a leaf, and Gulch's face was changing. Her grin was turning inside out. Her eyes were pivoting in terror. Her face was stretching and contorting and her black mouth was rolling wide open. She was trying to shout, but all that would come out

40

was "B-b-b-b-elinda." Then her mouth shut like a trap. Her knobby, needley legs began to move. She was fleeing the yard with the speed of a missile, abandoning the burlap sacks.

The wind carried Belinda closer to the ground, and she landed softly in the grass. She couldn't understand what had happened. She was relieved Gulch had left but afraid she might come back. Quickly, she worked to untie the sacks and let the children free. She had been waiting so long to meet them face to face. It was like a dream come true. Struggling with the knots, she imagined what fun they would have together. It felt as if she had known them for a very long time. But when the children finally crawled out of the bags, they didn't seem happy to see her. In fact, they seemed afraid.

"Don't worry," Belinda comforted, "Gulch is gone. You're safe now, but we ought to go somewhere else. She could come back."

The twins huddled close together both as pale as chalk. "Are you a good ghost?" Jerry squeaked.

"Don't get her mad," Jill whispered between clenched teeth. "She probably doesn't know she's D-E-A-D! Ghosts don't have brains. They can't think."

"I'm not dead," Belinda told her. "And I do have a brain! I wouldn't be able to speak with you otherwise, would I?"

But what Belinda failed to realize, as she hovered over Gulch like a falling leaf, and now as she stood before Jill and Jerry, was that she did not look anything like a living human being.

"I can see right through you," blurted Jerry. "You must be a ghost."

"Ixnay on the oastgay!" Jill said, elbowing her brother.

Belinda extended an arm and looked at it. Jerry was right: she could see right through herself, just as if she were cloudy water or smoky air. "I don't understand."

"Now you've done it," Jill said.

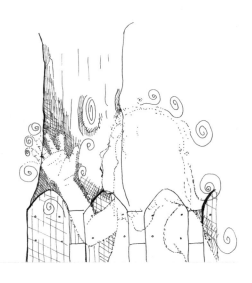

"I'm not a ghost...really. I'm a girl. My name's Belinda and I live in the attic room, up there. I saw you were in trouble, and I used my imagination to get me out of the room to help you. Something's wrong, or...." Belinda looked at her arm again. "Or, maybe you see me like this because you don't believe I'm real, because I can do things you don't believe real people can do."

"Why should that make a difference?" Jerry asked. "We can't change things with our thoughts."

Belinda smiled. She knew very well how the imagination could transform things. "Will you try an experiment for me"? she asked.

"Sure," Jerry said, "we love experiments."

"But we don't want to do anything that might upset you," Jill added emphatically.

"Good," Belinda said. "Please sit on the grass and look at me." The twins followed her instructions.

"Now, I'd like you to think with all your heart that I am a child, just like you. I am not a ghost child, but a real child. Do you think you can do that?"

"Oh yes, I'm sure I can," Jill said.

"My name is Belinda, and I am a real girl."

"Of course you are!" Jerry said.

"Of course you are!" Jill said.

"Very real," Jill added.

"Frightfully alive," Jerry put in.

"I am a real girl," Belinda stated again.

"As real a girl as I am," Jill said.

"Even realer than me," Jerry said.

The three carried on in this fashion for quite a while, and Jill and Jerry both began to grow tired.

"Don't give up yet," Belinda said, "just a bit more steady believing is all it takes."

Jill and Jerry renewed their efforts, and within moments Belinda began to flicker as if she were a light bulb.

"Keep believing," she said, "something's happening."

Jerry bit his lip, as though he were trying to lift something very heavy. Jill's face was turning quite red with the effort.

"We do believe, we do, we do."

Belinda could feel her body grow heavier. She could feel her heels sink deeper into the grass. "You're doing it!" she shouted.

She extended her cloudy arm and watched it grow denser and denser.

"Look, she is real!" Jill cried. "She is real!"

"But it can't be!" Jerry said in astonishment, "It's impossible."

Belinda felt her body lose some of its substance. It happened so suddenly, it hurt.

"Oh, look what you've done!" Jill scolded. "Now she looks like a ghost again and it's all you're fault."

"I'm sorry," Jerry said. "It's just so...I don't know...unbelievable."

"Try again," Belinda encouraged. But the twins were so exhausted they couldn't continue.

"Later," Jill sighed, "we'll help make you real later."

"But I am real!" Belinda protested. "I'm as real as you are."

Eight

ulch was in a terrible state when she stumbled through the door of the Dustbunny house.

"Call an exorcist!" she screamed. "That demon Belinda has gone and turned herself into a ghost. Now she's after us!"

"What on earth are you talking about?" Theodora demanded, her face black with the soot of the old fireplace she'd been searching.

"Belinda," Gulch cried, staggering towards her. "She's become a spook!"

"Get hold of yourself," Theodora said and thumped Gulch on the head. Gulch's eyes spun like the fruit in slot machine. "I saw her, I tell you. She attacked. I escaped, but she'll come after us again. I know she will, madam."

"I don't understand," Theodora said, grabbing her shoulders and shaking. "Does your brain need another wash?"

"No, Madam, please...."

"Make yourself clear then."

Gulch told Theodora how she had gone to the attic and seen the children and decided to snatch them as replacements for Belinda. She went into their yard and shoved them into burlap sacks.

"Very good, Gulch," Theodora purred. "So they're in the attic?"

"No...no, Belinda...the ghost, she came and...."

"You mean, you didn't get the other children?"

"No...I couldn't, madam...Belinda was...."

"You mean, you shoved the children in the sacks. They saw you, and you let them get away?"

"Well, yes!" Gulch said.

"So that would mean they can call the police and identify you? Is that so, Gulch?" Theodora's face looked hateful, but her voice remained as sweet as a candy jawbreaker.

"But the ghost," Gulch tried to explain, "she attacked."

Theodora turned mauve. "So what you're saying, Gulch, is you let those children get away, just like Belinda. In other words, you failed again, in other words, you've put me and the master at terrible risk, is that what you're saying?"

"Please, don't make me go back," Gulch begged, falling to her knees.

"You don't want to go back?" Theodora asked sweetly.

"No, madam. I'm scared."

"You're scared, poor Gulch. Well, you can do something else for me then," Theodora whispered.

"Anything...."

"You can clean all the dirty, grimy, dusty floors in the entire house."

"Gladly, madam," said Gulch. "You are so merciful."

"Yes, I know I am."

"I'll get my scrub brush and bucket and start right away." Gulch was as pleased as a puppy with a biscuit.

"Not so fast, Gulch," Theodora said, gripping Gulch's ratty hair and pulling out a fistful. "Not with your scrub brush. I think not! I want you to wash and wax all the floors with your tongue."

You might think this was a terrible torture, but it was only mild compared to what Theodora was capable of dreaming up. In fact,

Theodora devoted at least four hours a day to thinking up punishments and jotting down the really nasty ones in a little black book she had specifically for this purpose. Gulch got off lightly this time and only because Theodora felt mildly excited about kidnapping the children herself.

When Cedric returned home that evening, snarling and growling without Belinda, Theodora wasted no time in telling him her plans.

"She let those two perfectly good children escape. The stupid hag really believes Belinda's a ghost, imagine?"

"Fool," Cedric spat. "Anyone knows that old parlour trick. It's done with mirrors."

And if anyone should know anything about moldy old parlour tricks, it was Cedric, for once he had been a very bad magician.

"I say I slip out next door tomorrow afternoon and snatch them myself," Theodora said.

"What, and make me miss all the fun?"

"You always have fun! You get to humiliate and punish people all day long, while I just have Gulch, and she's little amusement anymore."

Cedric pulled at the bitten ends of his moustache and shot Theodora a pestiferous glance. "You know that not getting my way makes me unhappy," he said.

Theodora winced. "You don't like me when I'm miserable, do you?" he asked, reaching for one of Theodora's most prized meat-eating plants.

"Put Poopsy down this instant!" Theodora commanded. Cedric paid no attention.

"My Poopsy," Theodora squealed.

Cedric hurled the spiny plant across the room. Its pot shattered as it struck a wall.

"Oh, go ahead then. Have all the fun yourself." Theodora scuttled to collect the mangled plant. "See if I care!" She lifted the plant gently into the palms of her hands, and almost soundlessly began to weep.

Nine

Belinda knew she couldn't convince the children she was real, no matter what she said. Her experiments with imagination had taught her if you don't feel something is true in your heart, all the pretending in the world can't make it so.

But she wasn't going to give up either. She knew it was only a question of time and familiarity. Once the children knew her, she was sure they would believe she was real.

"Can I stay with you?" she asked them. "I'll help you clean your room and put your croquet set away." She knew they had trouble being tidy because she'd sometimes watched their mother picking up their things in the yard.

"Oh, that would be wonderful!" Jill said, but Jerry looked unsure.

"Why don't you go back up there?" Jerry asked, pointing at the attic. "Isn't that your home?"

"Not any more," Belinda said firmly.

"Of course you can stay with us. You can sleep in my room with me. Mother put bunk beds in my room in case I ever had a visitor. The top bunk's never even been slept in."

"But what will Mother say?" Jerry asked. "What will you tell her?

'I have a ghost I'd like to share my room with, is that fine?' She'll crawl the walls. You can't possibly ask her."

"Well then, I won't!" Jill said, "and neither will you!"

"You can't do that. It's dishonest. You have to tell her."

"I think Mother would want us to help someone in trouble, don't you?" Jill asked.

"Yes, of course she would, but...." Jerry began.

"I think it would scare Mother to think there was a ghost in the house, and I think it's wrong to scare Mother, don't you?"

"Why, of course, of course, but...."

"And when everything simmers down and Belinda finds a place to live, then we can tell Mother all about it. So it's not really like lying at all. We will tell her. Just not right away."

Jerry stood with a finger on his head. He knew he had some

objections, but couldn't remember what they were now. Jill was always tangling him up.

"Well, if you're going to do it, that's up to you, but I don't...."

"And, of course, Mother would expect you to be helpful too, Jerry," Jill added.

Jerry just shrugged his shoulders.

"Thank you," Belinda said. "I'm so happy. We're going to have so much fun together." But suddenly her see-through smile fell. Just because the children were going to let her stay with them didn't mean any of them were safe. The image of Gulch bobbed in her mind like an inflated balloon. A chilling seriousness crept into her voice. "But first, we must make ourselves safe."

"Oh, Belinda, do you really think that old monster will come back for us?" Jill asked, trembling.

"I can't be sure," Belinda said, but in her heart she was certain someone was coming.

"I think we ought to tell Mother about the monster," Jerry said. "Then she can phone the police."

"I think that's a good idea," Belinda said. But when Jerry and Jill did tell their mother about Gulch, she didn't believe them at all. "How many times have I asked you not to bonk each other on the head with those mallets of yours?" she asked.

"Perhaps if we hadn't told Mother she was a monster," Jill suggested afterward.

"Perhaps if we hadn't told Mother what she looked like," Jerry added.

"Well, there's no use trying to convince her if she doesn't believe it in her heart," Belinda said, wearily dropping her head in her hands.

"We'll have to think up a plan," said Jill.

"Lay a trap," Jerry agreed.

"Maybe," Belinda said, "but let's do it tomorrow. It's getting dark and I'm tired."

She yawned and stretched her almost transparent hands over her head. She was looking forward to hopping into the clean crisp sheets of the inviting bed, and when she did, she found the softness of the mattress even nicer than she ever possibly could have imagined.

Ten

edric had Limburger cheese, onions and soda water for dinner, then hobbled outside to his rickety porch for his usual belching hour just as the sun was setting.

He always thought better when he was being rude, and of all the complicated schemes he'd considered so far, the best scheme seemed to come now, while his loud, echoing belch was withering trees and shrubs, and petrifying stray animals who warily wandered around the crumbling old fence that encircled his property.

"Eureka...BURP!" he spluttered, "no need to get all knotted up!" His voice was loud and noxious. It didn't matter that he was alone — he liked to hear his own horrible voice.

"I'll just go in...BURP...and take those brats...BURP...is what I'll do...BURP!"

He'd thought before of offering something they couldn't resist, such as bribing them with chocolate. He'd even thought of secretly following them to the playground and telling them their mother had taken ill. But out here on the porch where the fizzy soda water puffed him up like a peacock and his rancid breath made him feel all-powerful, he decided to just walk right into his neighbour's house and take the children.

"Why shouldn't I?" he snickered, "I want them...BURP!" A small sapling fell to the ground like a black lettuce leaf. "Why shouldn't I take what I want!"

He stuck his chest out and tried to pull in his sagging stomach.

"In the dead of night, when everyone's sleeping, I'll crawl through a window like a burglar," he gloated. "I'll snatch those children like peas from a pod. They won't even know what hit them...BURP...until they wake up in a strange place."

He laughed raucously. The fence posts shook. A bewildered dog, blinded by the odour of his breath, fell into a gutter and howled.

Cedric chewed on his moustache and hobbled back and forth on the porch.

"I'll go in and collect one brat. Then I'll go back and collect another. What stupendous audacity! Going into the house twice. You really are delightfully devilish, Cedric," he chortled.

He lit a smelly old cigar and belched again. "And how they'll scream and cry when they discover they've been snatched. Oh, it's just too wonderful. And when they see Gulch? Ha...."

He tossed the dead match into some dry brown bushes by the porch. He was almost completely happy, except for one thing. And that one thing made him tug at his moustache with his teeth, as if he were a cat with a rat tail.

"Belinda," he muttered. He didn't know if she was with them or not, but he certainly didn't like the idea she'd turned crafty and was practicing parlour tricks.

If the police had shown up at his door, he would have welcomed them. "My poor little daughter Belinda. Ah, she must have fallen from the attic into the yard next door. She's always playing there when we tell her not to. She must have bumped her brain, and now can't recall her dear old dad." He would have told that story to the witless police.

"Oh, she must have had terrible dreams," he would have said, "dreams of being locked away. Dreams of a monster called Gulch. Oh, my, my, my."

He'd planned it all and was sorry the police didn't come. If they had, he was confident he could have convinced them. He thought he even could have convinced Belinda his lies were true. But with her out there, he couldn't be certain of anything, and the only thing he mistrusted more than one child was a group of children together, whispering, giggling and telling secrets.

It was always so much easier to sneak up on children when they were unaware. "Still," Cedric reassured himself, "I'll slip them away when they're sleeping, and they won't even have a chance to run. And if that Belinda brat's with them," he decided, "I'll make a third trip through their window." He laughed like an explosion. "I'll carry her off as well. What utter audacity! I am wickedly brilliant, no mistake." He puffed deeply on his cigar and belched a stinging smoke cloud out into the peaceful world.

Before Cedric knew it, the moon was bright in the sky. He shuffled across the creaking porch floorboards and butted his cigar under his foot. The lights in the windows next door shut off, one by one.

"Just a few more minutes," he said, wringing his hands in excitement, walking down the rickety, rackety porch stairs to the cobweb-covered garage where he retrieved a dusty flashlight and a rusting crowbar. He turned on the flashlight. A dull, thin beam trickled from it, straight into a cracked corner where three brown hairy spiders, each as large as a child's fist, scuttled for cover.

"You won't get away from me," he chuckled, drawing in his breath, and then letting out a tremendous belch that shook the garage roof. The belch, more lethal than insecticide, blew the three spiders onto their backs, dead as doorknobs, and from the garage rafters, a fine sprinkle of insects fell like snow.

Cedric's laughter ripped through the night. It filled him with glee to think of all the insect families he'd demolished with one burp. Dead bugs mingled with the dandruff on his shoulders. He didn't bother to brush them off.

Crossing his driveway, he moved through the bramble bushes at

the side of his house. The soft grass in the yard next door felt strangely uncomfortable to him. He limped along the yard, past the old oak tree till he came to the back of the house where he slid the straight end of the crowbar between the door and its frame. The lock broke with a pop. He pushed the handle and walked in.

His teeth clenched in a tight smile and the corners of his tiny eyes wrinkled like scars. He'd get those children, and no one would stop him. Then he'd sell them all to the rich sailor who wanted slaves to cook all day and all night in the galley of his boat, or the nasty old dowager who was looking for child servants, or the obnoxious farmer who needed farm hands. In the last few years Cedric's contacts with the rich and disreputable had increased. There was much more money in selling older children into slavery than selling younger children into families, and far fewer returns.

Had he not snatched Belinda when she was just a baby for a wealthy, indecisive couple who thought they wanted to buy a daughter? Did they not change their minds and never show up with the money? They never even let the Dustbunnys know. Theodora was beside herself with rage. That's when Cedric decided on doing things differently. Gulch would be the child's nursemaid. She'd raise her and keep her contained. When the child was big and strong enough to work he'd sell her as a slave. There was so much more demand for slaves than sons and daughters, and the misery it brought the children gladdened his heart.

In fact, Cedric had just been finalizing the sale of Belinda when the contrary child vanished, but another child would do just as well. Two children would be a bonus — and if Belinda happened to be among them, and he were able to retrieve her also, what an unexpected prize.

Eleven

ill and Jerry fell asleep as soon as their heads touched their pillows. Their mother fell asleep almost right away as well. But Belinda didn't seem to be able to sleep easily, though she was tired. Every time she began to dream, she jolted awake.

"What could it be?" she wondered, automatically clearing her mind for an answer. "What is it?"

Cloudy, dark, ugly swirls materialized in her mind. She half expected to see Gulch's face appear, but there was something different in this ugliness — something even more horrible.

She didn't want to look at it, but it forced its way into a persistent picture. It was the picture of an ugly man with dead bugs on his shoulders — a man she vaguely recalled. "Who are you?" she muttered quietly, "what is it you want?"

She saw his jaws clenched in a grin and the horrible cat-claw crease at his eyes. Then she felt her probing mind being sucked into his head, into his skull.

She tried to shake herself free, to recover herself, but the suction was strong and rapid. It was like she was being pulled over a waterfall. She saw him moving closer and closer to the room. With tremendous effort, she calmed herself. She allowed herself to feel the softness of the bed and the cool cleanness of the sheets. She allowed herself to breathe the freshness of the night air.

Still, she was in the current, but the current was not moving. It was like the point in an arm-wrestle when everything comes to a halt and, for a moment, the two opponents find themselves, forearms-flexed and equally matched.

Belinda's thoughts raced far, far from the current, even though she sat within its motionless swirls. The sunshine climbed into the sky and tiny white morning glories opened to greet it. Belinda was here — in a magic world of life and beauty, a world so real that once it must have existed for her. And then with a shriek, the current twisted like a steel beam. Belinda was jarred out of her magical world and back into Jill's room just in time to witness the bedroom door fly open, and a grimacing, greasy man break in.

Jill's breath was a steady hum in the bunk beneath. The horrible man's sharp eyes immediately fell upon her, and his greedy hands reached for her sleeping form.

"Mine," he chuckled, his disgusting breath filling the room.

Belinda felt her heart pound and her breath leave her. She wanted to run from this man, from his mind's black hole, but she couldn't leave Jill.

She leapt from the top bunk and floated gently down to the ground. Moonlight rippled through her as if she were a crystal. She'd forgotten herself completely.

She grabbed Cedric by his greasy hair, but her fingers slipped. He hadn't seen her yet, but now, turning in annoyance, as if she were some plaguing fly, his hard, cold eyes seemed to melt.

Belinda couldn't have realized what Cedric was seeing. She had forgotten what she looked like — and now, with the moonlight directly behind her, sparkling beams of colourful light through her, she appeared to Cedric even more frightening than a ghost — an avenging angel, prepared to drag him off and punish him for every crime he'd ever perpetrated.

His face turned the stark white of Jill's nightgown. His lower lip trembled. He dropped Jill back into her bed, as if she had become a flame. He fled from the house in terror, still mindful of making no noise, and tore through the moon-drenched night to his own front porch, where the remains of his cigar still smouldered.

Jill woke with a jolt. "I was dreaming a dreadful dream just now," she said to Belinda. "I was dreaming I had fallen into a vat of smelly onions and Limburger cheese, and I couldn't get out. It was awful! By the way, what are you doing down here?" she asked innocently.

Belinda didn't want to scare Jill but knew it was important she be prepared. The two collected Jerry from his room, and brought him back with them so together they could all keep watch for the rest of the night.

"He's got something to do with Gulch, and I know he'll be back," Belinda said. Her words possessed a strange certainty that made the twins shiver. "I don't know how or when, but I know he's not going to give up."

Twelve

e've got to collect my thoughts is what we've got to do," the distraught Cedric told Theodora and Gulch, who had both been awaiting his return. "Right now, they're all over everywhere. We've got to put two and two together!"

"Six?" Gulch offered quietly.

"No, you idiot. Not six. Not even four!" Gulch cowered.

"How are we going to get those blasted brats when an angel's with them?" demanded Cedric.

"That's not an angel you fool, it's Belinda! I don't know which of you is the bigger idiot, you or Gulch" Theodora drawled. "One of you swears she's a ghost, the other an angel. What we need to do is offer those children something no child can resist — hold it out to them, and when they put their hands around it, grab them."

"Shut up!" Cedric snarled. "I'm running this show, and don't you forget it."

Theodora puffed. "Look at you, you're afraid of your own shadow."

"Shut up, I said. I have to think." Theodora grinned and rubbed her long polished nails on the sleeve of her shimmery night robe.

"If it is a trick, I've never seen it before," Cedric muttered. "Of course it's a trick, what else could it be?" Theodora said.

"Well if that brat's going to play with magic, I'm going to show her a few tricks she hadn't counted on. Gulch, get my old black top hat from my trunk in the closet...and be quick about it, I haven't got all night."

Gulch scurried to the hall closet. The door rattled and creaked with age. Inside there was an old steamer trunk.

"I'm afraid I can't open it, sir!" Gulch said, fighting desperately to pry apart the trunk's rusty lock.

"Oh, get out of the way, you useless bag of nothing. I'll do it," Cedric muttered, limping toward her, gnawing his moustache.

Moths fled from tatty old coats that hung in the closet. Cedric kicked the steamer trunk. A pall of black dust spread from the trunk across the entire room.

"Ha!" Cedric laughed, singeing a few frightened moths with his still toxic breath. "Once a magician, always a magician," he said, smacking the side of the trunk again and mumbling some magic words.

The trunk lid flew open and hit the wall. Old brittle paint cracked like a mirror. "Eureka!" Cedric shouted, extending one arm, and bowing.

"So what!" Theodora called from the couch. "You think you'll get those brats with tricks?"

Cedric's mouth formed a grin. His yellow teeth glistened. He dug into the trunk and withdrew his old, worn magician's hat.

"What's the big deal?" Theodora continued. "It's just your tatty, mouldy old hat. I tell you, we ought to get a puppy. Little beasts can't resist other little beasts!"

"It's not the hat," Cedric grinned. "It's what's in it!" He thrust his hand into his hat, just as if he would pull a rabbit out, but instead out came an ancient black book. Theodora recognized it right away.

"No!" she shouted. "You can't. You swore you'd never use that book again. You promised you'd burn it. Not after what happened in Albuquerque."

Cedric grinned malevolently. "I changed my mind," he chuckled.

It was a large, black, musty-looking book, much larger than the hat. Scrolled across the front and side in swirly gold lettering were the words, "Black Magic."

"You can't be serious," Theodora choked, her face drained of colour. "You're mad!"

"Of course I am," Cedric laughed, "hadn't you noticed?"

Maybe Cedric dug out that old book because he was afraid of looking silly, or maybe it was just because his heart was foul and very bad. Whatever the case, it's safe to say things would have turned out far better for him if he'd left well enough alone. When people practice black magic, no matter who they are, it hurts them.

It doesn't matter if they are wicked grown-ups or just naïve children who stumble upon it accidentally. Black magic is like a boomerang: it flies out into the world to smack people in the face, but inevitably flies back behind you, and cuts off your own head.

If Cedric was as smart as he was mean, he would have known this. But his brain was very small. And, as is often true of small-brained people, he was convinced he was brilliant — so brilliant, in fact, he could control anything, including black magic.

"Albuquerque, pshaw," he said to Theodora. "I've learned by my mistakes!"

But, unfortunately, not enough to stay away from black magic or burn his book. To run from the merest whiff of it. He hadn't understood that black magic is like acid; it burns dark holes in your soul long after you've stopped using it; it corrodes and corrupts everyone it touches, every tree, every flower, every beautiful cloud.

It was a long time ago in Albuquerque that Cedric had first used black magic, and the story of his apprenticeship, I'm afraid, is very grim. Theodora and Cedric both worked for a kindly circus owner when they were much younger, Theodora as a lithe tightrope walker with pink satin shoes, and Cedric as a dashing young magician. They met in the circus and married there in front of a crowd of thousands. Mr. Santori,

the circus owner, gave them a large party and presented them with a brand new trailer all their own. "Isn't it marvy, Cedric?" said Theodora who was used to sharing an older trailer with an acrobat. "Look at the kitchen! It's even got a dishwasher!"

Cedric clumsily pulled a bouquet of flowers out of his hat. "Nothing but the very best for my poopsy!" he sang.

Not long in their marriage they were blessed with a child, a son they named Elmer. Now you might think that it must have been awful for the poor child. But, back then, Cedric and Theodora weren't even a fraction as nasty as they were to become. They used to take Elmer for long evening strolls in his buggy, and when he began walking, they played catch, and hide-and-go-seek with him. They loved Elmer as much as any parents can love a child, and even though they weren't wealthy, they tried to give him everything he wanted, and this is where the trouble first began.

"Me want ice cream!" the tiny Elmer declared whenever the phone rang. Bells reminded him of ice cream trucks, and every time he heard one, he would say the same thing.

"Just a minute, lambchop sweetums," Theodora would sing in his direction as she answered the phone.

"Me want ice cream now...right now...WHAAAAAAAAA!" he would cry, and Theodora would tell whoever had phoned she couldn't talk as she had to fix Elmer an ice cream cone.

Soon, friends stopped phoning. But Theodora really was too busy with Elmer to notice.

At night, Elmer decided he didn't want to go to sleep. "Me stay up all night and play with toys," he announced.

"But Elmer," Theodora tried to reason, "it will make you sick if you don't ever sleep."

Elmer was so insistent and Theodora so indulgent, though, that he got his way. The following day he was very sick, and Theodora was very tired, for she didn't dare go to sleep while her baby was awake.

Cedric, meanwhile, was working as many hours as Mr. Santori would give him. Before Elmer was born, he would do five or six shows a week. Now with Elmer demanding so many toys and treats, Cedric asked for more work hours.

"You'll wear yourself out!" Mr. Santori said. "Go home, spend time with your family."

"You won't give me more shows?" Cedric shouted. "Then I'll just go find someplace else to work."

66

Mr. Santori didn't want Cedric to go somewhere else. Even if he wasn't the best magician in the world, he had been a part of Mr. Santori's circus for a long time. "But what do you need all this extra money for?" the circus owner asked. "Babies don't cost that much to look after."

"You obviously know nothing about children," Cedric snarled.

Mr. Santori, who had eight children of his own, said nothing. He gave Cedric four more shows.

Now it would be easy to blame Elmer for all the unpleasantness I am about to relate. If it hadn't been for his whining, it's unlikely there would have been any unpleasantness at all. But Elmer was only a tiny child who had no idea of limits. Tiny children don't know how many hours it takes to earn enough money to buy one toy, let alone the hundreds that Elmer had cluttering the trailer. Tiny children don't realize their parents have feelings and needs too.

If only Theodora and Cedric had told Elmer right from the start that he couldn't have everything he wanted. If only they'd made it clear to him there were limits, he would have been a much happier child. But because they didn't, because they pampered and spoiled him, poor Elmer didn't know what limits were. He demanded more and more each day, and became madder and madder when he didn't get what he wanted right away.

After performing non-stop all day long, Cedric would drag himself to the trailer with a gift for Elmer in his hands. His eyes were bloodshot, and he was exhausted. There was seldom much for him to eat, as most of their money went on treats, toys, and special food for Elmer.

"We need more money," Cedric would shout angrily. Often when people don't get enough sleep they get cranky. "I need more shows!"

Mr. Santori refused to give him any more. "I'm sorry, Cedric," he said, "but the shows you're doing now aren't as good as they used to be. You're tired. You need a rest, maybe a little holiday!"

"NO!" Cedric screeched, "I want more shows! Give me more shows, or Theodora and I leave."

He'd never spoken to Mr. Santori that way before, and Mr. Santori was mad, even though he knew Cedric was tired.

"All right," he said. "You want to find someplace else to work, go ahead. I've tried to help you, but if you feel you'd be better off someplace else, go."

"Tried to help us," Cedric grumbled to Theodora that night. "Whatever did he do to help us? He works me to death, and he calls that helping? Why, he should have been paying me more money to begin with. He should have made allowances for the fact we have a child now. He's a stingy, nasty man, and he'll be sorry." Hatred welled up in Cedric like a toilet bowl overflowing.

Here was the very seed of evil, and the true beginning of Cedric's involvement with black magic. From this point on in his life, goodness began to drip away as if he'd sprung a leak. And his hatred and rage only grew fiercer.

Perhaps if he'd been aware of what was happening, he could have stopped it from getting any worse. Maybe, in time, he could have reversed the entire process. But evil chisels away at you very slowly. It begins when you hold onto anger and hatred, when you vow to get even with someone, instead of simply walking away. It contaminates your friends. And once you have stumbled onto this dismal path, you can only be certain it leads to misery.

Cedric began looking for another job. He was certain a magician of his talent and experience would be snapped up in an instant, but he found no one to hire him.

"It's that Santori," he growled at Theodora, "he's told everyone not to hire me. Well, I'll show him, and I'll show all those other losers too. No one's going to get away with treating me like this."

Mr. Santori said nothing to anyone about Cedric and Theodora. In fact, he hoped Cedric would find another job quickly, for it tortured him to see a young family struggle.

Still, Cedric blamed him for all his misfortune and began thinking about him all the time, thinking of ways to hurt him.

When you begin working with evil, whether you do so intentionally, or start by accident, you find evil opportunities arising everywhere. Cedric's big opportunity came when he met a magician called Condor.

Condor just showed up at the trailer one day, as nice and pleasant-looking as a distinguished gentleman can look. He had a white beard that reached to his top shirt button, quite well-tended, and his hair, when he took off his hat, was also white, but for a jagged line of black that ran down the centre like a lightning bolt.

"May I come in?" he inquired of Theodora, who was trying to calm Elmer. Condor rang the doorbell, and Elmer was insisting on ice cream, but there was none left in the freezer.

"Oh yes, do," Theodora said flustered,

"Elmer...Elmer...dear...Mummy will get you some ice cream, just as soon as ever she can."

Elmer threw a toy truck at her head. "Me hate you," he wailed at his mother. "You stink-pot," he roared, and tears of anger and frustration shot from his eyes like water from a sprinkler.

"Quite a spunky lad," Condor chuckled, reaching into his top hat. "What kind of ice cream would you like, son?" he asked.

"Me like chocolate, peanut butter, marshmallow with strawberry shortcake peppermint cookie," he sobbed.

"Oh, Elmer, there's no such kind!" Theodora said.

"Whhhhhaaaaaa" Elmer howled.

"Here you go, my lad!" Condor said, producing a scrumptious looking ice cream cone. "Just what you ordered."

Elmer couldn't believe his small red eyes. He toddled over to Condor and grabbed the ice cream — without saying thank you, of course.

"Yum..." he gurgled, "goodest ice cream. Give me man's hat, Mama. Me want man's hat!"

He was getting ready to scream and shout all over again, when all of a sudden his eyes got very heavy, and he couldn't hold onto his ice cream anymore. To Theodora's astonishment, he fell suddenly fast asleep.

"I don't understand, he never falls asleep like that," she said to the stranger. "How very amazing...."

"Perhaps he just wore himself out. A bright, spunky lad like that I imagine must burn up a lot of energy," he offered. When he smiled, his perfect white teeth glittered as if they were jewels.

"Why, thank you for the ice cream," Theodora said. "That was so kind of you." She wiped her hands on her apron. "It was an excellent trick, as well."

"Why, thank you," Condor said, bowing theatrically. "But actually, I didn't come to perform. I came looking for Cedric the Magnificent."

"I'm afraid he's out trying to find a job. I hope he gets one today, or I just don't know what we'll do. Elmer's destroying the trailer, and we're down to our last bread crust."

"Well, Madam, you needn't worry about that. If your husband's agreeable, he shall be working tonight with me."

Theodora was thrilled. So thrilled, in fact, she didn't ask any questions. "I'm sure he'd jump at the chance," she said eagerly. She didn't even ask Condor his name.

If she had, it probably would have meant nothing to her anyway, but when Mr. Santori heard a few days later that Cedric the Magnificent was working for Condor the Superexcellent, he was wild with guilt and despair.

"It can't be," he cried. "Condor is an evil man," he shouted through Cedric and Theodora's trailer window. He'd knocked on their door, but they wouldn't let him inside.

"Evil my foot!" Cedric shouted back. "You are the evil man, Santori, and you will pay for the way you've made me and my family suffer."

Mr. Santori didn't often cry, but when he went home to his own trailer that evening, he couldn't stop weeping. He had long ago heard about Condor and the way he harnessed the forces of evil to satisfy his greed. He wrote a letter to Cedric, begging him to return to his circus, but Cedric just laughed when he read it.

"That old Santori thought I'd come crawling back to him, but I didn't. Now he knows what he's really lost."

Cedric was quite happy working in Condor's show at first. Condor did not work for any circus, but arranged shows privately. He told Cedric he was using him as a back-up act to inspire the audience.

He paid Cedric a good salary and kept him working all day long. The more hours Cedric worked, the worse his act became. He had no time to develop anything inventive or original. His act was as stale as a piece of last year's birthday cake, as mouldy as a damp muffin. He was too proud to realize Condor wanted him and his act because it was so lousy, and in comparison made Condor's look extra-fantastic.

And finally, the day came when the audience had had enough of Cedric's stale fumblings and booed him off the stage.

Cedric wondered how it was Condor could do just as many shows as him and draw bigger and bigger crowds. It was unnatural. It couldn't be that Condor's shows were always fresh and exciting.

He found himself a seat in the audience in the shadows. He tried to notice what the audience was doing, how the audience responded, as it waited in anticipation for Condor the Superexcellent to perform.

People seemed breathless as they waited. But he overheard some talking about his act. "My dear," a well-dressed man said to his wife, "I really do believe that first act is Condor's way of giving us a bit of a giggle before he rivets us to our seats with his amazing talents."

"Yes," the woman said. "Just like him. Always tricking one way or another, but I feel rather sorry for that first clown, what was his name? Small Pox?"

"Oh, you are a card, my dear. Seedy Rick, I think."

The couple burst into laughter. "But really, dear, you'd think he'd know he was being made fun of, wouldn't you? I know if it were me, I'd want to hide away, and never show my face again."

Cedric felt the blood in his face rise. It crawled to the roots of his hair. Was that how the audience saw him then, as a clown? And could it be true that Condor planned it this way?

The heavy red velvet curtains parted, and Condor stood before his audience, looking bold and full of energy. Although he was much older than Cedric in years, he looked far less used. His face was smooth and handsome. There were no grey bags under his eyes or lines on his forehead. The audience cheered. Unlike Cedric, Condor brought nothing onto the stage with him. No collapsible wooden tables or little white ping pong balls, or even a magic wand. The only magician's prop he had was his glistening black top hat.

He began speaking to the audience in his deep, smooth hypnotic voice. "I understand from a weather report," he said, "there might be a rain storm today."

"But there's not a cloud in the sky," shouted a woman from the audience.

"Maybe not in the sky, but have you looked above your heads, here in the theatre?"

To Cedric's amazement small, smoky clouds were gathering at the back of the theatre and rolling forward. There was a tremendous crash of thunder, and a bright flash of lightning.

The audience squealed in terror and delight, as hard drops of rain pelted them, and strong winds played havoc with their hair and clothes.

Cedric watched the wind grab hold of stopwatches and wallets, and whip them forward under the stage without their owners' noticing. Everyone seemed so involved in the marvelous show that they didn't notice for a second they were being robbed.

"They'll probably go home tonight, convinced a pick-pocket got their belongings," Cedric thought. "Well, serves them right!"

He felt anger and hatred surge through him. "And if Condor is getting this much money, he ought to be paying me more, and giving me time off too!" As he watched Condor's show, Cedric got angrier and more resentful.

Condor next brought the sun out to dry the audience. The crowd cheered louder than he had ever heard a crowd cheer, and he realized how silly and childish his tricks must look in comparison to Condor's.

Instead of pulling a rabbit out of his hat, a trick Cedric hadn't even completely mastered, Condor pulled out an entire room of miniature bedroom furniture and then made it grow to full size before everyone's eyes.

He lay on the bed and levitated it, he sat on a stool and made it disappear. But most fascinating to Cedric was how he put himself right into a dresser mirror. It was a most astonishing trick. How could he vanish so completely and leave only his reflection?

"It must be a trick mirror," Cedric told himself, infuriated. "But where did it come from? Where did he learn to do these tricks?"

And then an evil idea flickered into his mind: "I'll steal all his tricks. I'll go out on my own, and become the richest magician in the world!"

Just at that moment, the audience got to its feet, roaring with applause and whistling its approval.

Cedric felt his energy draining, taken by the clapping crowd and transported upward to the stage. He could actually see the audience losing strength and finally in exhaustion collapse back in their seats. They looked used up, like marathon runners at the end of their race. They wanted to clap more and more, but couldn't.

Condor bowed on the stage as long as they clapped. He seemed to be growing revitalized and even younger-looking with the applause. His teeth glistened brighter than diamonds.

The audience staggered out of the theatre, weak and depleted.

"That was some show," Cedric overheard people saying. "I'm trembling, I feel weak. It really was the most amazing show."

Cedric felt weak and trembly as well; his body shook as he merged into a line leaving the theatre. But there was one part of him that was not weak — a part that seemed to have gained a good deal of strength from the show — his anger and hatred.

It bubbled and broiled and steamed in him. It made him sweat and sigh, and loosen his tie. "So Condor's a crook, and he's been using me as a fool. Well, we'll see who's the fool!"

He crept very quietly around the theatre to the back stage entrance. He snuck in unseen and waited. Every second felt like an eternity, but Cedric stayed put until he saw Condor moving down the backstage stairs, moving with a bulging sack over his shoulder and a victorious grin on his face.

Cedric tiptoed after him, following a bit at a time, hiding at the top of stairwells so Condor couldn't see him. He half expected Condor to leave the theatre. He'd never stayed before to see where Condor went when his show ended. But Condor didn't leave. Instead, he did a most unusual thing. He muttered some strange words, and a solid stone wall melted away to nothing.

"It can't be!" Cedric thought, for he knew the incantations magicians use are merely for the effect of the performance and have nothing to do with the tricks at all. Why was it Condor muttered one now? And why was he performing tricks after the show was over?

Cedric rushed after him, getting beyond the wall just before it re-materialized. Upon the walls were glowing candles housed in metal cages, and wide stone stairs leading downward. Cedric hid in the shadows and watched Condor descend. When the echoes of his footsteps disappeared, Cedric slowly and cautiously proceeded.

What he beheld at the bottom of the stairs took his breath away — an entire room of money and jewels and pocket watches glimmering like goldfish.

Condor stood just a few feet away, measuring out the contents of his sack. Cedric was afraid to breathe. He was afraid the slightest move would betray him.

"Such saps," Condor chuckled.

Dusty jars lined heavy shelves all around him. After he finished with the valuables, he moved towards the shelves. He opened a fresh-looking jar and put his fingers inside. Turquoise-coloured clouds ran into the jar like smoke from the ends of his fingers, and the sound of an audience's ear-splitting applause rumbled through the chamber.

"Got you!" he growled, slapping the lid on fast, before the smoke had a chance to escape. The applause instantly stopped. Condor laughed at his success. "Not one stray clap," he commended himself.

Cedric tried to figure out what Condor was doing, but he was not yet wise to the ways of evil, although the very seed of it was growing in him at an alarming rate.

"Must be some other trick, but why is he performing tricks without an audience?" he wondered. "It doesn't make sense."

Condor thrust his hand into his top hat and pulled from it the dollhouse-sized bedroom dressing table and mirror he had used in his show. He muttered an incantation, and just like it had done in the show, it grew to life size in seconds.

He surveyed himself in the mirror as if he were checking his face for something. It was quite dark in this underground chamber, but being so close Cedric was able to see him lean right up to the mirror and reveal holes in his face.

The bloodless holes were just slightly larger than the holes a pin might make in plastic, but when Condor pulled at them he could stretch them wide apart, and you could see that underneath them there was nothing but blackness.

Cedric's blood went cold. He didn't know what type of person Condor was, but the few remaining good instincts he had left were telling him quite loud and clear to get out and away as quickly as possible.

And perhaps, if it had not been so awkward to do so at that moment, he would have. Perhaps he would have gone and never thought about Condor and his magic again. But he was afraid he

could not get away without being spotted, and so he remained
huddled in a shadowy corner, watching everything.

Condor opened a dresser drawer and retrieved a dark metallic
bottle. It looked well used, but Cedric could just make out what the
handwritten label said: "Liquid Skin." Condor applied it to his face and
arms with the speed of experience. After he was finished, he stretched
his skin again, but all the holes were gone. He yanked his shining teeth
out of his mouth, and dropped them into a fizzling glass of clear fluid.
When he pulled them out again, they looked exactly like pearls. He
shoved them back in his mouth.

And then another most startling thing happened. From the bottom of his dresser, Condor withdrew a dusty old black book. Cedric strained to see what was written on it but couldn't make it out. Condor set the book on the top of the dresser and turned to a marked page. There were large golden symbols on the page.

Condor recited words, at first slowly and carefully, as he circled round and round the room, but then quickly and loudly. Sparks jumped from the book, higher and higher as Condor's voice grew louder. It was as if there were an electrical outlet short-circuiting, and its sparks were reaching Condor.

He began to quiver like gelatin; he twitched and jerked and jiggled. His face made funny expressions. His arms extended, as if he could not control them. The hair on his head began to fall to the ground and feathers — large black, brown and white feathers — began bursting their way out of his clothes.

Right before Cedric's eyes, Condor was transforming, but into what? Cedric couldn't quite make it out. His nose was growing sharper and more pointed. His face was turning red. His long white beard was winding around his throat like a fuzzy collar. His feathery arms were getting longer and his body was getting squatter. And, suddenly, Cedric realized Condor was becoming a gigantic bird.

Thirteen

edric knew very little about birds and nothing at all about condors, the very large type of vulture that his employer had just become. He was overwhelmed by the magician's transformation, and seeing the size of this bird, whose wings spanned almost the entire chamber, he grew dizzy. The bird blinked, shook its wings, and in a moment, vanished. Cedric took a deep breath and steadied himself. For a long time he remained in the shadows, fearing the bird might return, but after some time had passed, he crept cautiously into the room.

When he had first followed Condor into the chamber, he thought he would just follow him out again. But now it seemed that there was no way out, and he was afraid, not only of being trapped in this dungeon, but terrified of being discovered. If Condor had the power to transform himself into a bird, there was no telling what he might be able to do to Cedric.

Cedric approached the spot in the room he had last seen Condor. "There must be a trap door around here someplace," he assured himself. Then he caught sight of the strange black book open on the dresser, its pages full of the oddest symbols.

He was attracted to the book and his hands reached for it magnetically. He lifted it carefully, brushing the cover free of dust and soon the faint golden words, "Black Magic" appeared, just as if his hands had drawn them forth from the inky void. His heart hopped excitedly. So that was the secret of Condor. His tricks weren't merely magician's tricks; they were real magic. He had heard of such things, but never truly believed real magic existed. In all the years he had been a magician, every inexplicable thing he had ever seen had turned out to be some kind of a trick.

His eyes grew hooded and small. The book was large, but he shoved it under his cloak and proceeded toward the stolen loot. He crammed as much money and jewelry into his pockets as he could fit and then began examining the numerous jars resting upon the musty shelving. Written in neat black handwriting on each were the words "Audience energy" followed by a specific date.

He recalled the exhaustion he felt after Condor's show and moved closer to one of the jars to read the very small print: "To be used in one-eighth portion to paralyze, stultify, or combust." On another jar, he read: "Highly explosive, for supernovas, earthquakes, and volcanic eruptions."

Instantly, Cedric realized what Condor had succeeded in doing. Instead of making energy grow by sharing and circulating it with an audience, he had captured and preserved it all for himself.

"How wonderful!" Cedric sang. "I'll be the richest, most powerful man in the world! My troubles are over! I'll rule the universe! I'll call the shots! I'll be every president and prime minister, every king and ruler. This is my world now!"

He danced around in circles gleefully, clutching the horrible black book to his heart.

"If anyone gives me any trouble, I'll stultify them. If some country sends an army after me, I'll shake them up with an earthquake, or sizzle them with a volcanic eruption. Oh, happy, happy, lucky day!"

Cedric couldn't have known he was behaving like a fool. If he had sat and thought for a minute, he would have realized Condor would have made himself the most powerful man in the world if he could have done so. But I'm afraid if he'd even thought about that now, which he didn't, he would have probably said something like: "Condor is not even a quarter as bright as I am." For Cedric was thinking very much of himself at this moment.

He opened the book of black magic to the back and looked through the index where nasty spells of all kinds were listed.

"First, I'll take care of Condor and make sure he never returns," Cedric muttered.

He found a spell for "spontaneous combustion" and used the magic words from the book. He scooped out one-eighth part audience energy from the appropriate jar and quickly slammed the top back on. There was a great whooshing noise, as if some invisible dam had broken.

"I guess that takes care of that," he said, wiping his hands, eager to try another spell.

"Let me think, what else can I do?" and then impulsively he shouted: "Santori! I promised I'd get even with him, and get even I shall!"

He looked up "Get Even Spells" in the back of the book. "This time, I think I'll try stultifying," he muttered. Again he read the magic words and followed the incantation. He added one-eighth portion of audience applause. "Very handy stuff," he said.

This time there was a thunderous crash as he finished the last word of the incantation. The crash was so violent that Cedric found himself hurtling through space.

Yellow, stinking smoke clouded his vision. He was finding it difficult to breathe and was flying at such an alarming rate he had no idea where he was going, or if he would land at all.

When the smoke finally cleared, he was no longer in Condor's chamber, but outside the theatre, in a parking lot. He jumped to his feet cursing. "I must get back." He rushed into the theatre, positioned himself in front of a wall, and cried "Open Sesame," but nothing occurred.

"Abracadabra," he called next, but still nothing happened. "Jelly bean," he shouted, but the wall remained fixed. He continued this way for hours, calling out random words, but finally grew tired.

"To think I had the whole world at my feet and now I've lost it all," he wept.

He staggered out into the parking lot again. The sun was just beginning to set, and the entire sky was painted a strange flaming orange. Tears stained his cheeks as he traversed the lot. There seemed nothing for him to do now but go home.

Then, out of the corner of his eye, he spotted something black and tattered. A small sharp gust of wind rising suddenly flapped it open with a smack. Could it be the book of black magic, he wondered, holding his breath? He stumbled in his effort to retrieve it and picked it up reverently. He reached into his pocket for a handkerchief to wipe it clean of small stones and dirt. His hand failed to grasp his handkerchief right away, and for the life of him he couldn't figure out what obstructed his reach. But then, he remembered — the treasure he'd stolen. He'd gotten away with some of it at least. Things weren't as bad as they'd seemed after all and now with the book he might even find a way back into Condor's chamber, but search as he might, there seemed no such spell.

As he walked home, he consoled himself. "So what if I can't get into that secret chamber. I have enough money and jewels to live on while I'm learning how to get the whole world for myself!"

By this time, of course, Cedric was entirely confined by the stranglehold of black magic. He'd didn't consider any of the damage he had already done, as black magic has a way of kidnapping your conscience.

The bright orange sky rippled like a burning ocean above him. It never occurred to him how peculiar a night it really was. Some people who lived in the area swore it had been caused by a monstrous bird circling the sky who turned into a ball of fire and dropped to the earth as ash. In any case, Cedric never saw Condor again.

As for poor Mr. Santori, he fell asleep that afternoon and did not wake up. When he was found, he looked as if he were having a most peaceful sleep, for if black magic killed him, he was too good for it to spoil the beauty of his heart.

Cedric returned to his trailer, feeling quite elated. He rushed up the steps, bounded through the door, and was about to tell Theodora all his news when he saw she was sitting in a rocking chair, weeping.

"Don't cry, Theo, our problems are over forever. Look what I have here," he said, dropping jewels and fifty-dollar bills on the table in front of her.

She blew her nose and tried to stop her sobbing long enough to speak, but there was a lump in her throat and she couldn't seem to say anything.

"Where's our boy?" Cedric asked, looking around the quiet trailer. "Come to Daddy, Elmer. See the lovely money and jewels Daddy has!"

But Elmer didn't come. Theodora's sobs grew more and more inconsolable.

"Where's our Elmer?" Cedric demanded. "He hasn't come down with the flu, or anything like that, has he?"

Theodora shook her head, still unable to speak.

"Tell me, will you?" he asked, "where's my boy?"

Theodora pointed out the window.

"He's run away again?" Cedric asked. "Don't worry, he'll come back now I have some money. Have you called the police?"

Theodora could only shake her head breathlessly for the sobs were coming in torrents. Eventually, she did calm down enough to talk to Cedric, and this is what she told him: It was late afternoon, and she and Elmer were sitting outside the trailer playing on the grass with a ball. It was such a glorious day she saw no harm in getting a little air. She thought it would do Elmer good. They were having such a wonderful time together, and then she noticed something strange. Elmer seemed to have picked up some long grassy strands on his fingers. "Elmer, let me take you inside and wash your hands," she offered.

"No! Me want to play ball," he had insisted, and so Theodora let him.

But a few minutes later, these stringy grassy things had grown thicker and longer. Theodora tried to pull them off, but he screamed and cried as if it hurt.

She rushed to pick him up off the ground to carry him into the trailer and wash his hands, but when she tried to lift him he squealed in agony. She saw to her horror that these stringy grassy things were on his legs too, and, worse still, they were burrowing into the soil.

"Get up Elmer, stand up!" she told him panicking.

She watched her baby painfully try to disconnect himself from these horrible ground-hugging vines. He whimpered and cried and screamed, and there was nothing she could do to help him. He ripped himself free, and pulled himself to his feet. Tiny green shoots sprang from his fingers. She noticed his soft chubby legs had grown crusty brown, and he teetered on them for only a second before he changed totally from her child Elmer, into a small elm tree.

Cedric began to search his black magic manual from cover to cover to find a way to bring his baby back. He trembled when his eyes fell upon this short paragraph right at the beginning, which he had skimmed past before: "For every good you remove, you will lose something of great value; for every evil you remove, you will gain a portion of that ill. These are the laws of black magic, and all that attach to it can neither be undone nor reversed."

"What have you done to our child," Theodora cried. "It was you, and that horrible book. Take it and burn it. Throw it in an incinerator," she cried, pushing Cedric as if she would like to see him burn along with it.

But Cedric and Theodora would never be the same after this. When they looked out their trailer window and saw the small elm tree swaying helplessly in the breeze, they couldn't endure it.

Theodora began to grow as bitter and evil as her husband.

Before long, she'd forgotten Elmer's face and was saying to Cedric, "I'm sick of looking out this trailer window at that tree. You've got some money, so buy me a big house — and make sure there are no elm trees in the yard. I simply can't abide them!"

And so they moved into their dusty, leaky, creaky house where they allowed themselves to grow more and more evil and forget more and more about Elmer and the black magic book — until this day.

Now, Theodora stormed off to her bedroom. "You'll be sorry!" she shouted at Cedric, leaving him to flip through the book's pages.

"I remember Condor once performed a piece of magic that was most amazing and would come in useful now," he said completely ignoring Theodora's warning. He turned to the book's index. "Yes, here it is!" he announced and chuckled.

"What is it, sir?" Gulch creaked. She was curled up in a corner like a spider.

"None of your business," he said, shielding his book from her eyes. "You get off to bed. You need as much beauty sleep as you can get."

"But perhaps I can assist you," she offered, her mouth twitching ever so slightly.

"You? Help me?" Cedric yowled. "Oh, that's a good one! The only way you can help is by getting out of my sight."

Gulch slithered up the stairs, but not all the way up. She stopped midway, crouching so she could watch Cedric without being seen.

She watched him limp back and forth, gnawing at his moustache, occasionally furrowing his brow. And then, finally, he set the book down on the coffee table, muttered some curious words and vanished completely.

Gulch cautiously crept down the stairs. She scrambled to

where Cedric had stood. There was a smell in the air of rotting eggs. She leered at the book and then let her eyes roll. She was thoroughly alone. Her hand shot out and seized the book. She shoved it under her jacket and then slithered up the stairs to her bleak room.

The floorboards groaned under her flat feet, and cockroaches crunched. She lit a candle, as she was not allowed an electric lamp, and sat on her bed, trying to avoid the rusty springs that cut through her mattress. Her fingers skimmed the list of spells in the book's index. Her wobbling, wiggling eyes tried hard to focus. She was searching for something specific but, surprisingly, something that did not have to do with Belinda or the Dustbunnys. She was searching for a spell for herself — a spell that would make her beautiful.

"If I were beautiful," she muttered, "everyone would love me! If I were beautiful, sir and madam would treat me differently."

She peered at the writing but couldn't discern much in the darkened room. She squinted, moving the book closer to the flame. Gulch had not even seen the end of the book touch the wick of her candle. Her wheeling, wobbling eyes were too busy searching for a beauty spell. She'd combed all the b's in the index for beauty, all the p's in the index for pretty, all the c's for cute, even the h's for handsome, but had found nothing. If she had been more familiar with the book, she would have known that it contained no spells to create beauty, only ones to destroy it. Now the book flared and sizzled with freakish black flames that ran like small tickling fingers over its pages.

"Oh my!" Gulch croaked, as the blazing book spilled from her hands. It fell with a flash, spitting choking green clouds all around her, and when she moved to smother the growing conflagration, the black flames spread like a spider's web across the floor. Small pockets of fire appeared in the room's corners, bright red tongues of heat licked their way to the tops of the walls, the tatty curtains at Gulch's window turned to ash, and swirled like grey snow through the dense air.

"Oh my!" Gulch croaked again, as she scurried from the room.

Fourteen

Belinda and the twins decided to take turns keeping watch. That way they figured they'd all get a chance to sleep, but because they were all so wide awake, it didn't work out that way.

"Let's tell each other stories," Jill suggested.

"That would be good," Jerry agreed. "Do you know any stories, Belinda?"

"Can you tell us the story of how you came to be stuck in that scary old house next door?" Jill asked.

"No! Tell us about your parents!" Jerry demanded.

"I'm afraid I don't know enough about either," said Belinda sadly, "but if you'd like me to make up a story, I'll try."

"Please do," Jill begged.

"Yes...do!" Jerry added.

Belinda sat up and tucked a blanket around her feet. She licked her lips, took a deep breath, and began.

"Once upon a time, I was a very small baby...."

"Of course you were," Jerry interrupted. "We were all small babies once!"

"Give her a chance, Jerry, she's just getting started," Jill said.

"I was a very small baby," Belinda continued, "and of course, like all small babies could do nothing for myself."

"Of course!" Jerry huffed.

"But I had a wonderful mother and father. They were happy and loving. They did everything for me. Even when I was too small to speak, they read me stories and sang to me."

"Sounds like our mother," Jill said.

"Yes," Belinda continued, "and I loved them very much and was very sad when...when...."

"When what?" Jerry asked.

"When..." Belinda said, feeling words lodge in her throat "when...the others took me away." Long wet streaks glistened on Belinda's transparent face. She felt a strange crackling noise inside her head.

Jill and Jerry watched helplessly. "Oh, Belinda," Jill said, "don't tell us this story. You're crying!"

"What?" Belinda asked, getting up to look in Jill's dresser mirror and seeing there the strangest frothy white tears melting down her cheeks.

"What can we do to help you feel better?" Jill asked. "Please tell us what's happening." Now if Belinda hadn't been so shaken herself, she would have been able to tell the twins every small change she was experiencing. She would have been able to tell them about the crackling sound inside her head and the stinging rush of soapy tears that she felt shifting like a blocked damn. She would have been able to tell them that a locked secret room in her head had sprung open, and she was discovering things there which had been lost for years.

"I was taken away," she wept. "Two horrible people stole me and washed my mind with...with dish soap, so I'd forget my parents. I was locked in that attic room and left all by myself." Belinda's bubbly tears drenched the bedsheets.

"Don't think about it," Jill advised. "Don't think about it if it makes you cry."

"But it's good for me to cry," Belinda said, "don't you see? The tears are washing the soap out of my brain. I'm starting to remember!"

"But maybe it's better if you don't remember," Jerry said. "If you remember, it will only upset you!"

But Jerry had never known the horror of losing his memories. He had never known the agony of not knowing, nor felt the gnawing, persistent pain of rumbling memories longing to be found.

Soapy water continued streaming from Belinda's eyes as she remembered beautiful days spent in the shade of a graceful oak tree. She was only a baby, no more than two. Her parents were somewhere close by, she was sure, but then, out of the dark cold shadows something ugly crept up on her and snatched her. She had been too young to fight or scream, but she recalled with a shiver the feeling of cold rough hands on her tiny arms.

She could hear a conversation in her head now, one she had witnessed but had not understood. A gruff man's voice saying: "We'll keep her until she's old enough to sell as a servant. We obviously can't count on want-to-be parents."

And the angry shriek of a woman: "Gulch will have to look after her then, because I'm certainly not going to." The woman dragged small Belinda by her ear to the kitchen sink and filled the basin with hot sudsy water.

Belinda remembered being submerged. She gulped and gurgled and thought she would drown. Water was poured directly down her ear, and she felt the tremendous pressure. She fought against the brain washing the only way she could. She tried hard not to let go — especially of her mother and father. But even as she remembered this now, their images were only hazy.

"I can see the tiny house I used to live in," Belinda told the twins, "and my nursery with white lambs on the wallpaper and a mobile over my crib. I can see my favourite toy, a stuffed elephant. I called her Elli and carried her everywhere."

But, still, no matter how much Belinda could remember, the faces of her parents remained blank.

Jerry and Jill didn't know what to do or how to help.

"Just ask me questions," Belinda told them.

"Okay," Jill said, "do you remember a birthday?"

Belinda sobbed. She couldn't recall a birthday. Foam collected into puddles on the floor.

"If this goes on much longer," Jerry said, "we'll all drown!"

But neither Jill nor Belinda laughed; they were working too hard at recollecting.

"You must have had one birthday," Jill persisted. "You said you were two when you were snatched. You must have had at least one nice birthday."

Belinda thought hard, lines of tears and soap staining her face, until finally she stumbled on a memory. She was a baby, blowing out a single candle on a cake and clapping her hands. She wore a small party hat, and when she had extinguished the candle and looked up, there were two people smiling at her. Two jolly happy people with round loving faces. "My parents!" shouted Belinda. "I've found my parents!"

"What do they look like?" Jill asked.

"They look like they love me. They look like they care about me," Belinda cried.

Now it should be mentioned that people who have memories

always appear more real than people who don't. And without even knowing it, Jerry and Jill began seeing Belinda as a real little girl. Her small transparent body sunk deeper into the bed without their really being aware of it. Her skin became more solid, her body sturdier. Even her voice seemed to grow stronger.

Thick foamy blankets of tears covered the bedsheets now. But neither Jill nor Jerry cared. They just wanted to help Belinda.

"Tell us more about the horrible couple who stole you from the park!" Jerry said.

"I'd never seen them before," Belinda began, "but I have seen one of them since. He was the man in your room tonight, Jill! I knew he looked familiar! That must mean he's trying to snatch and brainwash you too!"

"How frightening!" Jill declared, shaking right down to her shins. "I would definitely not like to be brainwashed!"

"Me neither," Jerry echoed.

But someone nearby was intending to do precisely that just as

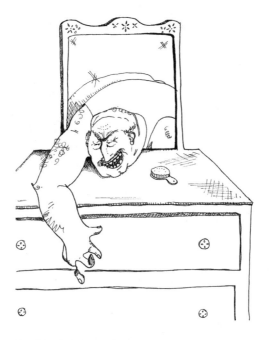

Jerry spoke. Cedric hurtled through space. He never would have guessed transporting himself with black magic could be so rough. When he'd seen Condor vanish, it looked simple and elegant. But there was a frayed underside to black magic that Cedric was only beginning to discover.

He jolted and jarred and felt his body creak and crack. He really wasn't physically fit enough for this kind of journey. But just when he felt he could stand no more of it, he arrived at his destination — Jill's dressing table mirror.

Ever since he'd seen Condor climb into a mirror, he'd wanted to do the same. But because he had promised Theodora to give up black magic, he'd never had the chance.

"Nothing to it," he muttered, getting up off of the floor's reflection, still aching from his bumpy flight. He positioned himself in the mirror so he was hidden, but could still see the children talking on the bed.

"Ah, so there's that brat Belinda, no longer an angel, eh? Well, I have a few tricks up my sleeve for her," he said as he rubbed his fingers together, which just in the last few hours had begun turning the same decomposing shade of black as the toes on his left foot.

He lay in wait for the children. Sooner or later he knew they'd come to the mirror and when they did, he'd reach out and grab them. But the children continued talking into the early hours. Belinda continued crying and remembering. Cedric sat back uncomfortably in the mirror. Patience had never been one of his strong points.

"It looks like that Belinda brat will need another brainwashing," he thought, "and this time it'll be thorough."

He waited and waited, but no child came to the mirror. The evil coursing through him made him more impatient than usual. He was eager to get back to the book. He knew there were a hundred things he'd like to do with it.

Time crawled slowly for Cedric, his fury mounting as he checked his watch again and again. He'd lost interest in Belinda's revelations long ago. Now his body was becoming stiff and cramped from sitting in one position for such a long time.

"Curse those brats," he silently huffed. The waiting made him itch, and when he went to scratch his shoulder, his black index finger fell right off. But that was only a minor annoyance. What was really making his blood boil was that Belinda and the twins looked so cozy all tucked up together in the bottom bunk, while he was miserable and scrunched in a tiny cold reflection in the corner of a mirror.

"Well, blast them," he finally said out loud with a finality that resounded.

Belinda and the twins instantly stopped talking and looked towards the mirror.

"It's just our imagination getting the better of us," Jerry said. "We're expecting to hear noises, so we do."

Now while this might be true of some children, it certainly was not true of Belinda. Belinda's imagination never got the better of her; she always got the best of it.

"I think we better check anyway," Belinda said.

But the three didn't have to check anything. They didn't have to move an inch, for right then Cedric began to climb out of the mirror.

"If you won't come to me, than I'll come to you," he said, sliding off the top of the dresser and onto the floor.

He really wasn't used to this kind of activity, nor was he used to sitting so long in one position. He groaned as he limped along toward the bunk beds in his shiny pointed shoes. He wagged a finger that dropped off his hand and fell to the ground.

"That is so gross!" Jerry said.

"Quick, push your bodies against the wall," Belinda shouted. "If he's going to try to get us, let's not make it easy for him."

The three shoved themselves fast against the wall. They were all on the lower bunk, and Cedric had to stretch and reach to get them.

Belinda smacked at Cedric's rotting fingers as they reached towards her like long black water snakes. Another finger dropped off and landed on the bed.

The twins squealed, and Belinda thrashed. Cedric grabbed and groped, he rolled and roiled; but nothing he did seemed to bring his stiff, bulky body closer. Every time he charged after them, they'd flatten their little bodies against the wall. He was simply too unfit to crawl into the bottom bunk and get them. Finally, he took one blind lunge and felt the reward of a child's thin arm in his grasp.

"I've got you now," he said, not knowing whom he had.

He began to pull, and then to tug as a child screamed. "Let me go!" she shouted. It was Belinda and she was remembering the first time he had grabbed her. She had been too young to scream and fight then, but now she would give him as much trouble as she could. She opened her mouth wide and sunk her teeth into his wrist. He yelled, jumping backwards, slipping in a puddle of her bubbly tears. His back hit the floor with a crack.

Fifteen

Fire!" Gulch called weakly. "Fire!" she said again. She was afraid she would be punished, so she didn't dare call much louder.

The fire in her room crawled from beneath her door, and began scaling the walls in the hallway. "Fire!" Gulch said a little louder, and cleared her throat. Green smoke twisted in front of her eyes. "Fire," she said. Then Gulch did something quite unusual. She straightened her suit jacket and went to knock on Theodora's bedroom door.

"I'm afraid I've started a fire in my room, madam," she said rather boldly. "I think we had better phone the fire department and evacuate the house."

Theodora was too alarmed to beat Gulch.

"Where's Cedric?" she demanded. "Does he know of this?"

"I'm afraid, madam, he's vanished."

"Vanished?" Theodora asked.

"Yes, he was looking in that book, and he just up and disappeared."

"Fool," Theodora said. If Theodora could have only seen him at that moment, lying flat on his back, unable to move a muscle, she would have thought him even a bigger fool.

Smoke began filling Theodora's room, swirling and puffing, twisting around both Gulch and Theodora like a fine green shroud.

Theodora frantically searched her closet. "Take this box," she commanded, handing a shoebox of crumpled papers to Gulch. "There are some very dangerous things in here that could land us all in jail, so mind they don't fall into the wrong hands. Guard them with your life."

Gulch took the box, scurried down the stairs and out the front door, while Theodora retrieved another large box from her closet in which she began collecting all her carnivorous plants.

Sixteen

s a fire truck sounded in the distance, the twins' mother, disturbed by the commotion, woke from a deep sleep.

She heard a scream and a thump coming from Jill's bedroom, and before her eyes had fully opened she was standing there asking, "What on earth is going on?"

She saw Cedric struggling on the floor, puddles of bubbly tears, and a cute little girl she had never seen before emerging from Jill's bottom bunk.

"I demand an explanation," she said, "right now...and make it good!"

It was four o'clock in the morning, and no parent likes to get up then unless it's absolutely necessary.

"This man tried to take us," Jill began.

"Yes, he tried to take us into the mirror," Jerry said.

"And this is Belinda, the little ghost girl," Jill said.

"She's really just a regular girl," Jerry said, "but we didn't believe it, until she cried and found her remembers."

"And this man," Jill said, "he was going to put dishwashing soap in our ears so we'd forget...."

And although their mother could not make head nor tail of their story she phoned the police right away, for it was clear the man writhing on the floor had intended no good. Both a police car and a fire engine screeched to a halt on the street out front at precisely the same time.

All the people in the neighbourhood left their warm beds and crowded in front of the Dustbunnys' house to see what was going on. The newspapers, radios and television stations showed up next. Cameras flashed, film whirled, people crowded and shoved to get a better view of the dark flames that rolled from the rickety rackety roof into the inky sky.

An ambulance arrived next, and Cedric was carried out of Jill's bedroom on a stretcher. "It wasn't just me, stealing children," Cedric snarled at the police as they questioned him, "It was that Theodora. She's the one that put me up to it. She's the mastermind behind all this."

Theodora struggled across the smoky front yard of her home, shielding her plants, when a policewoman discovered her and arrested her.

Belinda and the twins shivered as they watched the drama unfold from Jill's window, then they all looked at one another, thinking the very same thought: "What would become of Belinda now."

"I've got a brilliant idea!" Jill said suddenly, and dragged Belinda by the sleeve down past the front lawn, past the ambulance where Cedric was cursing, past the police car where Theodora was screeching, right in front of a T.V. camera. "Tell them what happened," she said.

Belinda went red in the face.

"Tell them what happened," Jill insisted again, "and maybe they can find your parents."

Belinda cleared her throat. "My name's Belinda," she began. The cameraman flapped his arms madly. A woman with a black notebook ran her finger across her throat. "Beat it kid," she whispered, "we've got a fire to film!"

"I used to live in the attic room of that house that's burning," Belinda told the camera.

"Great kid, now get out of here, before I get a technician to carry you away," the woman hissed.

"The police have just arrested the people who stole me. They stole me when I was only two-years-old."

The woman with the black notebook began to listen. She signaled the cameraman to keep filming.

"My parents have round faces and smile a lot. My mother has brown curly hair, and my father has short blond hair."

Another camera crew began filming Belinda. Some microphones were shoved in her face and people began asking questions.

"I don't know where they live, or what their names are, but if they are watching this on television, or hear about it on the radio, or read it in the newspapers, or if there's someone who knows who they are, please let them know I'm waiting for them."

Cameras flashed, Belinda's eyes tingled and by eight o'clock that morning, every newspaper, television and radio station in North America carried some story about Belinda and the Dustbunnys.

"Look," Belinda told the twins as she showed them the local newspaper headline, "we're all here." The headline read: "Brave Children Trap Kidnappers."

Jerry took the paper proudly and looked at the photograph. The three children stood close together before swells of people. "Well, it's not as good as some pictures mother's taken of us," he said, considering it until his eye caught something he hadn't seen. "Look at this!" he said pointing.

Belinda and Jill looked at the photograph again. Neither had noticed that right behind them, in a shadowy gulf of gaping strangers, the photographer had caught the twisted face of Gulch.

"My goodness!" Jill exhaled. "I thought they would have arrested her and put her in jail too."

"So did I," Belinda agreed.

"Do you think we should start worrying again?" Jerry asked.

Seventeen

ulch crouched in a pile of ashy wood, scratching at her warts and guarding the shoebox, just as Theodora had told her. The Dustbunny house was no more, and the police had taken both Cedric and Theodora.

"I wish the police had taken me away too," Gulch thought. She was cold and hungry and very afraid. It was a windy day, and a crumpled piece of newspaper blew across the street and affixed itself annoyingly to her jacket. When she removed it, she beheld a photograph that made her brain rattle. "Belinda!" she cried, feeling a strange stirring sensation rumble through her as she read how Belinda had been snatched. The sensation was not hatred, nor anger. It was a kind of a prickly feeling that turned into a sharp painful smack in the head. Rusty red tears began to run from her eyes. Her ears began frothing; even her nostrils bubbled.

"I'm dying," she wept, her eyes wobbling wildly as torrential tears washed a good portion of the woodpile away, and left her standing ankle deep in ashy, rusty, foaming water.

Because Gulch had been brainwashed many more times than Belinda, she dispensed gallons upon gallons more tears than Belinda had done, and suds still streamed from her eyes and ears. Bubbles formed in her throat, emerged from her mouth, and rose in the air like clear balloons.

She watched them sail above her and noticed, even though she

Our Daughter
is
MISSING

Genevieve
Call 298-1887 REWARD

wept, that her vision was improving. The bubbles sailed over bushes and trees, and as she watched them disappear, she remembered something of her young life, a time she had been given a bright red balloon. How she had played with it, trying to prevent it from touching the ground and keeping it airborne for as long as she possibly could. Other memories emerged too, lovely memories, of friends and parties and quiet happy times when she coloured and painted beautiful pictures all from her imagination, times when she felt cared for and loved.

A deluge of lather spilled from her ears with a splatter, and everything in her mind abruptly became clear.

"I remember my mother and my father. They loved me. They were nothing like the Dustbunnys. They cared for me," she sobbed. "And I can remember, I can even remember my address. I lived at 124 Green Street, and it wasn't far from here. That terrible Theodora invited me to her house to see a puppy, and then she dragged me in and made me stay. It was..." she sobbed, wiping the bubbles from her nose, "just over the bump in the road."

Still crying, Gulch mustered her courage and removed herself from what was left of the woodpile. She slithered through the street and hunched over the hill. When she saw the beautiful house she recognized as her childhood home, she began to run toward it. The first thing she noticed stapled to a telephone pole in front of the house was a tattered, yellowing poster of a small girl. The poster read "Our Daughter is Missing." Then she saw a kind looking woman come out of the door carrying dozens of other posters.

"You'll listen for the phone, Charles, in case anyone's seen or heard from her, will you?" she shouted into the house.

"Charles..." Gulch thought, "that was my father's name."

She rushed to the woman just before she got into her car. "How do you do," Gulch said, "I was wondering...."

"I'm sorry, dear, I really can't talk right now," the woman said nicely. "I'm looking for my daughter. She's been gone for so many years, but I feel certain she is somewhere close by, and I won't stop looking for her until she's found." She handed Gulch one of the posters. "Her name is Genevieve."

The name brought new tears to Gulch's eyes. "That was my name," she choked. "This picture is of me when I was little."

"Genevieve," her mother cried, embracing her. "Yes, I see the likeness. I would have seen it right away, but you've grown up, and I think I was still expecting to see a little girl. Oh Genevieve, where have you been?" she asked, holding her daughter close.

"Charles, Charles!" she called, trembling with joy, "it's our Genevieve, she's come home!"

To her parents, Gulch was not ugly because she was someone they loved. They had the warts removed from her hands and face, because a virus causes warts and can spread. They took her to a dentist and got her terrible, rotting teeth fixed. They gave her vitamins and put her on a healthy diet with lots of fresh fruit and vegetables, because they could tell by her appearance she had not been eating properly for years. Before long, her skin was a lovely healthy colour, and the black hair on her nose had all disappeared. The hair on her head became thick and luxurious, and she didn't slither and hunch when she walked. In fact, nourished with love, she grew very attractive. "I've done a lot of horrible things," she said one day as she sat at the breakfast table with her parents.

"Yes, Genevieve, perhaps you did, but you didn't mean to do those things. You were under the influence of some very nasty people," her mother said, patting her shoulder.

"Yes, that's true," she answered, "but still, I did do nasty things, and thought nasty thoughts, and I don't think I'll ever feel completely good about myself until I've put right what I can."

Eighteen

Belinda had not been as fortunate as Gulch. Because she had only been a baby when the Dustbunnys abducted her, she had no idea about street names and numbers.

"I'm sure if my parents were alive they would have seen my picture in the newspapers and come for me," Belinda told the twins sadly one day when they were playing croquet and she had the red mallet.

"Don't lose hope," Jill told her.

"Yes, you know if you don't feel they will come for you in your heart, they will never come!" Jerry said. "That's something you taught us!"

"I know," Belinda said, "but I really did think they would have come by now."

She was happy to be with the twins, playing croquet and eating ice cream, but ever since she'd remembered her parents' faces, she'd yearned for them.

When the croquet game was over, Belinda decided to stay outdoors and think. She sat on the cool carpet of grass. It had been a long time since she'd sat thinking. She focused upon her parents in her mind's eye.

"Perhaps my parents will come for me today," she said calmly, "perhaps they just might." She said it without a demand in her heart, but as light as a willow leaf. "Maybe they will."

The sky grew dark and overcast, trees shook, the lilac bush rustled furiously. Still, Belinda stayed, imagining her parents, asking for them to come for her.

"Get in the house, Belinda," Jill shouted out the back door, breaking Belinda's concentration. "There's going to be a big storm. You've got to come in now."

Belinda sadly stood. Now that she was free from the attic, it seemed her imagination didn't work as it once had. Yet, she was sure it was much better to be free.

She went into the house and sat by the window in the living room. She watched as tiny lines of rain lashed the window. The sky grew darker still, and the rain grew denser.

Soon, all Belinda could see through the window was a smudge of trees and grass. Everything was blurry. And down at the bottom of the path, she saw a man and a woman, dressed in raincoats with an umbrella.

The doorbell rang and the twins' mother went. "Can I help you?" she asked. Belinda heard two odd sounding voices with strange accents. She didn't even stir, she was too busy wondering where her parents might be.

"Belinda!" shouted Jill, who had followed her mother to the door. "Your parents! They're here! All the way from Australia!"

Belinda couldn't believe her ears. She flew to the door, her feet barely touching the ground. And when she saw those two happy faces smiling down at her, she thought she was having a wonderful dream.

"Don't wake me up, Jill," Belinda said. "Promise me you won't!"

"I won't," Jill laughed, "because you are awake, silly."

Belinda's parents hugged and kissed her. They spoke in a way that suddenly she recognized. "We never gave up hope of finding you, darling...never," her mother said.

"How did you find me?" she asked. "Did you hear about me in the news?"

"No," her father said, his hand tightly wrapped around hers. "There was no news of what happened to you in Australia. We got a letter from a woman called Genevieve. She told us where we could find you."

"Genevieve?" Belinda asked, "I don't know a Genevieve!"

"Maybe she just read about you in the paper. Some people just naturally do nice things," Jill said, her joyful grin so broad it hurt.

"But how would she know where my parents lived?" Belinda said. Her mother kissed the top of her head. "I don't know, Belinda. I'm just happy that we've found you at last!"

Epilogue

Belinda went to live happily ever after with her parents in Australia. She started school that fall, and made many, many friends. But she never forgot the twins, whom she pays visits to regularly, using her extraordinary powers of imagination.

A television network is talking about making a movie of her life.

Genevieve went on to do more and more naturally nice things. She was helped by the contents of the shoebox, which contained all the names and addresses of all the children Theodora and Cedric had kidnapped over the course of many years.

When she ran out of names from that box, she began hunting kidnappers down by posing as a rich woman who would pay any price for a child servant.

She has to date reunited more than three thousand kidnapped children with their parents and put over five hundred kidnappers behind bars.

Cedric and Theodora are still in jail, both suffering from the backlash of black magic. Cedric's fingers and toes continue to drop off as he chews his moustache and mutters, trying to recall the exact wording of Condor's disappearing spell. He has tried over one million seven hundred and fourteen thousand incantations without success, and has used nearly as many tubes of Epoxy glue.

Since seeing the black magic book again, Theodora has been unable to erase the memory of Elmer from her thoughts. She knits branch-shaped stockings and weeps, vowing if she ever gets out of prison, she will find Elmer and try to coax him into becoming a child again.

Biographies

Victoria/Vancouver author **MADELINE SONIK** is known for her two critically acclaimed adult works, *Drying the Bones*, a collection of short fiction, and *Arms*, a novel. She began writing *Belinda and the Dustbunnys* for her youngest daughter after the tragic and profoundly affecting disappearance of Victoria's Michael Dunahee. She says she needed to write a story that would show her daughter the tremendous power of the imagination to rescue and the tremendous strength of love to endure. All author royalties will be donated to Child Find.

GRANIA BRIDAL lives in a seaside house on Vancouver Island in Sooke, British Columbia, as close as possible to the ocean and the forest. She fits her art work intoa very busy life that includes bringing up two lovely daughters and surfing whenever and wherever there are waves. Grania has exhibited her work in Sooke and in Victoria. Her most recent exhibition was at the 2002 Sooke Fine Arts Show.